BBC

DOCTOR WHO

COMBAT MAGICKS

BBC

~~DOCTOR WHO~~

COMBAT MAGICKS

STEVE COLE

BOOKS

1 3 5 7 9 10 8 6 4 2

BBC Books, an imprint of Ebury Publishing
20 Vauxhall Bridge Road
London SW1V 2SA

BBC Books is part of the Penguin Random House group of companies
whose addresses can be found at global.penguinrandomhouse.com

Penguin
Random House
UK

Doctor Who is a BBC Wales production.
Executive producer: Chris Chibnall, Matt Strevens and Sam Hoyle

First published by BBC Books in 2018

www.penguin.co.uk

A CIP catalogue record for this book is available from the British Library

ISBN 978 1 785 94369 0

Typeset in 11/14.3 pt Albertina MT Std
by Integra Software Services Pvt. Ltd, Pondicherry

Publishing Director: Albert DePetrillo
Project Editor: Steve Cole
Cover Design: Lee Binding/Tealady Design
Production: Sian Pratley

Printed and bound in Great Britain by Clays Ltd, Elcograf S.p.A.

Penguin Random House is committed to a sustainable future for
our business, our readers and our planet. This book is made
from Forest Stewardship Council® certified paper.

MIX
Paper from
responsible sources
FSC® C018179
www.fsc.org

For Kamilah Chowdhury

Chapter 1

The TARDIS came tumbling like a gambler's die across the dark baize of the night. Its wheezing salute sounded through the sky and the light that crowned the police box shell shone out.

An unearthly golden glow pulsed and broke through the clouds. The TARDIS flew into it.

And screamed.

'Whoaaaaaaaaa!' The Doctor pirouetted away from the smoking TARDIS console, blowing at her fingers. 'She did not like that. The TARDIS did *not* like that.'

'Yeah, I noticed!' Graham clung to a crystal outcrop as the whole control room listed sharply. The usual warm orange lighting had become a demented wash of reds and purples, plunging the cavernous space into shifting shadows, and a bell was clanging somewhere, deep and dolorous, like the end of the world was coming. Graham stared round wildly to check that Ryan and Yaz were all right, saw a tangle of limbs flailing against the mushroom-shaped console and breathed a sigh of relief.

'What's going on?' Ryan yelled.

'We ran into something, thirty thousand feet above the surface of the planet below.' Walking against the wind as she slowly fought her way back to the controls, the Doctor looked like a mime artist, except her blonde hair really was blowing all about her face, her blue coat-tails flapping like they wanted to take off. 'A belt of energy. Ask me what kind.'

'What kind?' Yaz shouted.

'I have no idea! None! Isn't that brilliant?' The Doctor's grin was wide enough to swallow them all as she reached the console at last, twisting and tickling the controls into submission. The buffeting grew calmer, the floor began to level out.

Graham let go of a long, shuddering breath. 'Jeez, Louise, I thought we'd had it then.'

'We've landed.' The Doctor stared at the controls as if daring them to disagree, her tone somewhere between accusation and wonder. 'One day I'll get the hang of flying this thing …'

'You think?' Panting for breath, Yaz helped Ryan to his feet, letting him lean on her. But Ryan, unhappy accepting help from anyone, pulled away and tottered against the console. Smoothly he propped himself up on his elbows, as if the stumble had always been part of the plan.

Graham pretended not to notice so as not to embarrass him. 'Everyone all right?'

Ryan nodded, and Yaz pushed long black strands of hair back from her face. 'So, belt of energy, not good for the TARDIS …?'

'Not good for anyone in close proximity.' The Doctor was taking in whatever weird information her machine was prepared to divulge. 'Luckily this is AD 451 and human beings can't fly, so your ancestors should be OK.'

'History time!' Ryan grinned. 'Hey, Doctor – love saying this – where on Earth are we?'

She beamed. 'Gaul.'

'Gaul? What's that?'

'It's a place, mate,' Graham told him. 'Asterix came from there. In the comic strip.' Yaz and Ryan looked at each other blankly, and Graham frowned. 'You must know! Asterix the Gaul, feisty little fighting hero by Goscinny and ... thingie?'

Ryan shook his head.

'I was Goscinny's and Uderzo's inspiration, you know.' The Doctor pulled her hair over her lip to make a blonde moustache and winked at Graham. 'Almost definitely.'

'Anyway.' Graham affected a lofty look at Ryan and Yaz. 'I know Gaul and you don't, so I win. Old France, wasn't it, Doc?'

'You mean, *isn't* it!' The Doctor blew her hair away and grinned, rubbing her hands with glee. 'Gaul is out there on the other side of those doors, right now. Is! Right this instant.' She produced her sonic screwdriver and waved it over a crack in the console. 'And Gaul isn't just France! It's Belgium, Luxembourg, a fair bit of Switzerland and Northern Italy, *ein bisschen* of Germany and the Netherlands ... although actually, this bit we've landed in *is* old France. So, not *ein bisschen* but *un peu*.' The crack in the console widened, and she pushed her hand inside, teeth gritted as she groped at the space inside. '*Un peu de countryside*,' she went on, 'somewhere between Orléans and Chalons.'

'Euro road trip!' Ryan grinned. 'We going out, then?'

'Got to, haven't we?' Yaz looked towards the white doors of the police box; sometimes she'd caught them twitching, like they couldn't wait to open. 'I mean, that energy thing, all this time ago, it can't be natural, can it?'

'Not natural to Earth.' The Doctor pulled out a smoking cylindrical rod, crystal and laced through with wires. 'Look! Passing through it almost burned out the force-field generator.'

'So, you reckon this energy's alien,' said Ryan.

'It would be,' Graham muttered. 'Still, thirty thousand feet over the Earth, at least it's not hurting anyone down on the ground.'

Ryan shot him a look. 'What about birds?'

'Birds don't fly as high as that,' said Yaz.

'Tell that to your average Rüppell's griffon vulture!' said the Doctor. 'Actually, don't bother, at thirty-seven thousand feet they'll never hear you.' She snorted at her own joke. 'They soar for hours in the jet streams up there, getting all the oxygen they need despite the thinness of the air.' She grew more sober. 'Amazing how creatures can adapt to exploit their environment.'

Ryan nodded. 'I'm up for some adapting.' He started down the ramp to the exit. 'Let's get sightseeing!'

'Oi!' Yaz raced him to get outside first.

'Oh, come on,' Graham called after them, as they vanished through the doors, 'don't go charging off …!'

'Keep an eye on them, Graham,' the Doctor murmured, running the buzzing sonic over the glowing rod she'd pulled from the console. 'Just let me get this sorted. I'll be right there. Well, I'd be right anywhere, obvs, cos I'm always right.' She grinned at him. 'Right?'

'Right, boss,' Graham agreed. 'Always.' Steeling himself, he walked down the ramp after the others, into the unknown.

Chapter 2

It was a bad place for a tent, he thought. Too small a clearing, too far from fresh water, and little room here among the trees for a good fire. No decent forage to be had either, not for you nor your horse – although since thousands of the finest soldiers anywhere had churned the fields to mud under foot, hoof and cart wheel, God knew there was little enough food to be had in this whole backward area.

Bittenmane swayed and almost stumbled, and he placed a hand on his mount's long, broad head. 'Stay ready,' he murmured. That the horse could still support him at all was a miracle. Like him, he knew that Bittenmane must hold weariness deep in his bones, blood leaking from the stripes sliced into him. *But still we stand*, he thought, even when the burning night offered nowhere to hide.

He cast a sour look past the treetops, up at the endless burning ember of the sky, and hated that he was growing used to something so unnatural. But then he eyed the severed heads of old foes hanging from his saddle, and smiled grimly. *At least you're doing better than those poor fools.*

Weariness weighed on him, but sleep was out of the question this night. He forced himself to focus on the blue tent before him in this godforsaken spot. Yes, it was a lousy tent, he decided: too tall and thin, how could you sleep well in that? And where was the cart that carried it, and the beast that bore the load? Something had made the groaning roar that had led him to scout the area; he suspected a terrible monster, fire-breathing and hairy, conjured by the Romans' witch – a witch who must be far more powerful than his own. *His* witch claimed to be weakened by battle, unable to retaliate, but he didn't trust her.

'Death is nothing but a meeting place,' she'd said with such certainty, a tight smile on her crooked face. 'We shall all meet again in the next life.'

He shivered to remember her words, which had seemed more threat than comfort. He half-hoped that by now the scheming hag hung red and twitching from a Roman's sword, that devils had taken her before he or his men could follow her to the afterlife.

There was no sign of a monster here, and he wondered if that last blow to his head had affected his reason. But Bittenmane's ears lay flattened; he didn't trust the tent either. So when its doors opened, he drew his sword in a second and nudged Bittenmane into the thick foliage at the clearing's edge.

A woman came out of the tent, strutting with the confidence of a high-born. He stared, incredulous: her dark skin and the perfumes upon it spoke of exotic lands to the east. Her beauty was great: her hair long, her eyes black and her teeth white as pearls; she might have been Zenobia, long dead queen of Palmyra, reincarnated here beneath the magic sky. 'Whoa!' she said, though she had no horse. It was the heavens that held her transfixed; she gazed up as if God were waving down at her.

A moment later his hand tightened on the hilt of his sword as a young man came out: a man with cropped hair and black skin, that the Romans would call an *Aethiope*. He looked strong but bore no scars; his face was smooth as a child's. Did men not fight in Africa? The man wore no armour, only strange flimsy skins, and he too became fast transfixed by the sky. Perhaps he was a eunuch, and the girl's escort?

This theory was proved badly wrong as a third figure appeared from the big blue tent. Surely there was room for no more? This latest was an older, white-skinned man, who wore worry-lines like scars and a coat of strange leather. He placed a hand on the shoulders of the younger man and the woman, joining them in staring up at the sky through the heavy branches.

'No wonder the TARDIS went into one,' this older man said. 'That's what we rode through?'

'What is it?' breathed the woman.

'Freaky as hell,' the Aethiope whispered. 'Bet you the Doctor calls it beautiful.'

'Course she will,' the older man nodded.

These must surely be Romans, and yet they were babbling in his own tongue. Spies, then? Even if they weren't, their meaningless babble would surely lead the soldiers of Rome straight here. Either way, they had to die.

Raising his sword, he pricked the ribs of Bittenmane with both boots, and his horse lurched towards the strangers.

As one, the trio took their eyes from the sky, saw death charging them down, opened their mouths and screamed. He pulled back his sword-arm to silence all three cries in one great blow. But in a blur, another woman, pale and lithe, had pushed past his targets to stand before them. There was steel in her eyes and a rainbow blazed across her chest.

'Oi,' she said. 'No.'

The word was like an axe thrown at Bittenmane, who reared up, turned and threw his rider. The warrior struck the ground shoulder-first but managed to roll over and finish upright.

'Get behind me,' the woman told her followers.

He pitched forward, his sword swinging at her, the thick whistle of the blade as it parted the air sweet in his ears ...

But then heat filled his body and he was tossed backwards like a sack of firewood. *Who struck me?* The fearful thought lasted a moment in his head before he struck a tree and the impact raged through his spine. He lay, winded and terrified, staring about the clearing for ghosts. Bittenmane whinnied but the dark girl was soothing him, a hand on the horse's dark chestnut flank. Suddenly she backed away, groaning 'Ew! Eww!' at the sight of the heads hanging from the bridle; was she trying to ward off evil spirits, or attempting to raise them?

He watched as his sword was snatched up by the white-skinned man who gripped it awkwardly in both hands as if struggling with its weight, the boy by his side. Both looked to the woman with the rainbow, like slaves to their mistress for instruction. He saw that in her right hand she held a sort of metal wand.

'Wow!' she cried, looking up at the sky as if nothing had happened. 'Isn't that beautiful?'

'Told you,' muttered the black boy.

So. Another witch. Damn this modern world and its endless sorcery! Though this woman was different from the Tenctrama hags. She seemed more like a whirlwind descending from the high mountains, dangerous and beautiful, standing there with the others and yet somehow held apart.

Now she strode towards him; automatically he struggled to rise. 'No, no, don't try to get up. I didn't hurt you, did I? My bad.' The witch looked concerned, waved her wand. 'My force-field generator – er, I mean, my shield of air thing – it's a bit broken.' She tucked it into a flap of material in her strange coat. 'Sweet of you to try to fix it with that big old sword of yours, but the power lattice needs time to regenerate. Well, don't we all. What's your name?'

'My name … is Bleda.'

She knelt down beside him, her green eyes fixed on him like he was treasure, hands pressing against his face like a healing shaman. The softest, palest hands! Typical sorceress: she had never worked or struggled a day in her life. 'That's a big old cut down your cheek there, how'd you get it?'

11

'I am a soldier.' He shrugged. 'Each wound is a mouth that sings my valour.'

'Well, I love a positive attitude, Bleda. But this one's going to be singing 'Infected' before long. Great song, but you don't want wounds doing covers.' She smiled, but her eyes showed she was wary. 'How about I clean up your scratch while we have a nice cosy chat about why the sky's on fire?'

'I will not be mocked by a Roman witch.'

'I'm not a witch. And I'm not Roman.'

'You look like a Roman.'

'You should've seen my last face.' She grinned. 'I'm the Doctor. This is Ryan, that's Graham, that's Yasmin. If you stop trying to kill her, she might let you call her Yaz.' She pulled a small jar from her pocket and took off the lid. 'And *this* little beauty is a synthetic intelligent collagen that boosts the regenerative powers of your body a thousand-fold. Three millennia from now, you'll be able to buy it over the counter in any pharmacy! On Titan, anyway.'

'Ahh!' Ryan, the boy, nodded. 'She got it on Titan.'

'Graham's rash,' mouthed the girl.

'You make it sound dodgy!' Graham protested. 'Everyone gets rashes …'

'Anyway it's deffo not Roman.' The Witch-Doctor dipped a finger in the ointment from the jar and pressed it to his cheek; the wound tingled and then felt soothed. 'None of us come from Rome. At least, not lately.'

'Three of us are Britons,' added Graham.

'Why are you in Gaul, then? To sell your magicks?' He nodded to the sky. 'Rome has its own sorcerers.'

'So the name-calling's based more on observation than superstition.' Witch-Doctor put the jar back into her pocket. 'You believe in magicks because you've seen them with your own eyes.'

'These days, no battle can be fought without the Tenctrama.'

'Tenctrama? What's that, a weapon? A people?'

'Once, they were. Barely any of the witches survive now.'

'The Roman Empire battling with magic?' Graham stuck the sword point down into the earth and leaned against it. 'I must've skipped school the day they taught us that.'

'I don't think what's happening here is part of your established history. Something feels very wrong …' The Witch-Doctor pulled another wand from inside her coat; its crystal tip whirred as she waved it wildly at the sky like a shaman over bones. 'Yeah, there's something totally alien about that excitation field up there. The sonic doesn't like it …'

Small wonder the strangers' skins looked so soft: it was action that toughened a man's hide, not a child's endless gabble! But his own wound had scabbed over already; while this Witch-Doctor might speak madness, she truly had powerful magicks, both to harm and to heal. Plans stirred in the warrior's head …

'There are so many different tribes traipsing around Europe right now, but I've never heard of the Tenctrama.' The Witch-Doctor looked down at him. 'What are your lot, Bleda – Ostrogoths? Burgundians? Gepids?'

'We are *Hsiung-nu*,' he said proudly.

13

'Oooh, OK! Well, you're a long way from the steppes of East Asia. What are you doing in Gaul, sightseeing?'

'We are waging war.' He paused. 'The Emperor Valentinian has wronged our mighty lord Attila, so he and his people must pay in land and plunder.'

'Hang on.' Fear showed clearly on Graham's smooth, pale face. 'Did he say …?'

'Attila.' Yaz was nodding, wide-eyed. 'Doctor, he means *the* Attila, doesn't he? Attila the bloody Hun!'

Chapter 3

Yaz forced herself to meet Bleda's stare. Even as he smiled, there was a kind of cruel haughtiness about the exotic face and features. Beneath the conical leather hat, his long, thick black hair was matted with blood – perhaps his own, more likely from his victims. (She tried not to think of those heads slung about his horse like charms on a necklace. What were they, trophies? Something to show the kids back home?) His body was covered in tough but tattered leather armour, and the tatters of a richly embroidered coat of animal furs lay about him. Even injured and exhausted as he was, there was an aura of power about him that made Yaz feel uneasy. His eyes were never still, assessing, calculating; biding his time.

'What's the panic?' asked Ryan. 'Who's Attila the Hun?'

'Biggest, loudest and hairiest barbarian there ever was,' Graham put in. 'Rode around on a big horse killing people the whole time.'

Bleda seemed amused. 'Is that what they say in Britannia?'

'That's the caricature passed down by history.' The Doctor crossed to where Bleda's horse – a stocky, short-limbed animal with a head big enough to break down doors – stood at the edge of the small clearing. 'Attila is the warlord of a massive tribal empire that came out of what would be modern-day Kazakhstan.' She began to apply the gel from her little jar to the cuts and gashes scored into the horse's scurfy hide. 'Under him, his people – the Huns – conquered and assimilated everyone in their path.'

'All who live fear Attila,' said Bleda, still smiling. 'Your witch chooses strange words, but she is right on this.'

'Oi! I told you, I'm not a witch, or a Tenctrama, or whatever. I'm the Doctor.'

'You throw a man from his horse with a wave of your wand, and carry crystals that make sense of your surroundings!'

'Yeah, well.' Ryan shrugged. 'That's how we roll in Britannia.'

'We're just travellers,' Yaz said.

Uh-huh, she thought, *and 'just' is the right word*. Sometimes, here on the Doctor's dark frontier, Yaz wished she were still in uniform. Wearing it back in Sheffield had always made her feel more capable, strong, part of a team. Hair scraped back, hat in place, high-vis jacket over the black and white: she was marked out as someone who belonged anywhere, ready to help and with a right to intervene. The Doctor just breezed in and made the whole universe her business like she was born to it, and Yaz longed for that confidence. Here, though, in the ancient past – almost two hundred years before the Muslim faith had even been founded – it was harder to accept she had any real status beyond 'tourist'. And the idea that Attila the Hun *himself* could be nearby was just surreal.

The Doctor finished up with the injured horse, patted him gently. 'What's his name?'

Bleda grunted. 'Bittenmane.'

'Aww, that's sweet,' she deadpanned. 'Bittenmane's very alert. Who's he listening out for, friend or foe?' When Bleda did not answer, she turned to him. 'You know, I'm glad we ran into each other. Always good to get a bit of local knowledge. But I *am* surprised to find as important a leader as you left unattended.'

Bleda's innocence was smooth as the new skin over his wound. 'I do not understand.'

'Aw, come on! You're no simple soldier hiding out in the woods. You think we haven't noticed the posh stitching on your fur coat there, the silver and gold on your horse's saddle? All that bling makes you easy to spot on the battlefield – which marks you out as a military leader of some importance.'

Yaz continued the train of thought. 'And that wound on your face was fresh. You're hiding out from others who want you captured or dead.'

'Lower your voice, witch.' Slowly the Hun got back to his feet. 'I am Bleda, Commander of the Ten Thousand Horsemen, right hand to the king.'

The Doctor bowed. 'What went wrong?'

Bleda shrugged. 'For weeks we lay siege to the town of Orléans. But barely had the town surrendered to us when Aetius's rabble met us there in combat.'

'Flavius Aetius! Of course, Rome's *Magister Militum*.' The Doctor turned to her friends. 'Aetius is holding Rome together, the power behind the young Emperor.'

'And the Tenctrama – witches of the Goths and Alans – are the power behind Aetius,' said Bleda.

'The who now?' said Yaz.

'Did he say Alans?' asked Ryan.

'A tribe from Iran,' the Doctor said, 'migrated into Europe.'

'The Alans are powerful warriors,' added Bleda.

Ryan smirked. 'Are they, like, as powerful as the Nigels and the Kevins?'

'There's actually a tribe called the Franks,' the Doctor revealed, and Ryan laughed out loud. 'You've heard of the Goths, though?'

'Course. Bunch of them hang out at the bus station drinking cheap cider and looking mardy.'

'I used to go out with a goth,' Graham recalled.

Yaz nudged him. 'Is that how you got your rash?'

'Enough of this!' Bleda's eyes flashed, with power enough to silence them all. 'You ask for knowledge, then prattle when I would impart it!'

'Sorry.' The Doctor smiled sweetly. 'Do go on.'

'Without the Tenctrama's craft, the Romans would never have triumphed at Orléans. Even so, my men gave battle bravely and bought time for mighty Attila to escape with the bulk of our army.'

'With all the spoils.' The Doctor held up her little jar. 'How many of your ten thousand horsemen survived along with you? I'd like to help them if I can.'

'Most are dead now.' Bleda sniffed hard, cleared his throat and spat out clotted blood. 'In the end I took what able men I could and we withdrew under cover of nightfall ... fewer than a thousand of us, with Enkalo the witch alongside us for protection.' He shook his head. 'But the witch was useless! The skies caught light to show us in our retreat, and we were tired by combat, and legions fresh to the fight overtook us and closed around us in a pincer movement.' He shrugged. 'Perhaps a hundred of my men fought through and fled into these woods.'

'I'm so sorry,' said Yaz quietly. 'How long have you been hiding here?'

'With the moon eclipsed by fire, it is hard to be sure.' Bleda smiled. 'I don't know how many Romans followed us into the woods, but we make them work hard for our heads.'

'You mean, they're still looking for you?' Ryan wasn't smiling any more. 'Hunting you down like dogs.'

Graham glanced around nervously. 'So that's why their witches lit up the sky. So the search parties can see better?'

'Wait.' The Doctor pointed. Bittenmane was shifting his weight uneasily, big eyes trained on the edge of the clearing. 'I think someone's coming.'

'Who's there?' Bleda's deep voice carried into the eerie forest. 'Bleda, Commander of the Thousand Horsemen, fears no one.'

I thought you told us not to advertise who you are, you idiot! thought Yaz, but then a gory figure staggered into the clearing, panting for breath and clearly on the brink of collapse. His bloodied face was a real car-crash, sharp black eyes like little eggs lying in a nest of scars, the big, broken nose a crooked arrow pointing to the bared yellow teeth and a dark beard, parted and tied with plaits of coloured ribbon, that stretched down to his barrel chest. 'My lord,' he said weakly, 'my prince …'

'It is Alp. A noble chieftain, badly wounded.' Bleda crossed the clearing quickly but couldn't reach his friend in time to stop him sinking to his knees.

The Doctor was beside them in a flash, and Yaz joined her. 'He looks done in. Needs water.'

'He needs wine.' Bleda crouched and pulled a goatskin flask from his belt and splashed a sour-smelling liquid against Alp's lips, making the man splutter. 'Why have you left cover, Alp? Tell Bleda, your commander.'

Alp looked around, eyes clouded with confusion. 'You … have taken prisoners?'

Bleda dodged the question. 'These witches wish to help us.'

'Witches?'

Alp recoiled, his eyes wide with terror, and Yaz cringed as the dark, clotted split hacked into his chest opened. She looked at the Doctor. 'Healing gel?'

'I think it's too late to help him,' said the Doctor, but of course she was already pulling out the pot regardless.

'No!' Alp rasped, terrified. 'No witch will touch me!'

'Alp, you idiot.' Bleda took a swig from the flask himself, grimaced and then tossed it aside. 'Why are you here? I told you to stay hidden and wait.'

'I had to tell you.' Alp stared at him as if trying to bring him into focus. 'The Roman soldiers … have left the forest. Enkalo is slain.'

Bleda took the news like a cuff round the face. 'Slain?'

'Enkalo's your Tenctrama witch, right?' said Ryan.

'Enkalo stayed with us, for … "protection".' If a fifth-century barbarian had heard of air quotes, Bleda surely would've used them then. 'We have only her mistress, now: Inkri, who remains at camp.'

'I'm surprised Attila agreed to leave Enkalo with you.' The Doctor was searching out Bleda's face. 'He must value his commanders very, very much.'

'He values me most of all,' Bleda bragged. 'What happened, Alp?'

'The Romans dragged her from hiding. She did not resist. She did not scream when the life was hacked from her body. She only laughed. Then there was a great light. It flashed through the forest …' Alp gasped suddenly, twisted hard in pain, and the Doctor squeezed his hand until his body relaxed. 'The soldiers ran, calling to their brothers. They said it was time to leave the forest.'

'Perhaps it was poor old Enkalo that the Romans were after,' Graham suggested.

'Makes sense,' Yaz agreed. 'If your man Aetius has witchcraft on his side too, she was, like, competition.'

'Bump her off and the magic defences go with her,' was Ryan's elegant conclusion.

Alp took a fierce grip of his comrade's arm. 'I cannot die now! Enkalo's soul is waiting to take me. You heard what she said, that we'd all meet again in the hereafter …'

'Wait.' The Doctor's head was cocked to one side, as if she could hear something they couldn't. 'Can you feel it? Hairs on the back of the neck. No one else? Just me?'

'What's up, boss?' said Graham.

The Doctor looked at Bleda. 'The soldiers might have gone, but I don't think they've given up on you. Or, something hasn't.'

Yaz could feel it now. A tingling through her skin, like thunder was coming. There was a noise too, a low, rhythmic rustling, things beating at the air. Distant explosions of sound went off alongside: a man's scream, twigs snapping ... distant but getting louder. Closer. Bittenmane reared up, spooked, and turned in a tight circle.

'Come on.' The Doctor bent over Alp and put her hands under his armpits. 'The Romans didn't leave the forest, they evacuated it. Made way for something else to come and drive you out more effectively. We've got to get back to the TARDIS. Help me with the Huns!'

Ryan stooped to grab Alp's feet while Graham went after Bittenmane. Yaz almost gagged at Bleda's stench as she tried to help him up.

Then the leafy branches above them exploded darkly as crows and ravens swooped down in droves upon the clearing. Their black eyes shone in the unearthly light, and great beaks gaped and snapped as they fell upon everyone in the clearing. The Doctor dropped Alp and pulled out the force-field generator – but the curved blades of a raven's beak knocked it from her grip. Yaz gasped and covered her head, doubled over, terrified. The huge birds were everywhere, flapping over her, biting and scratching. The assault was overwhelming. Yaz fell to her knees, the air thick with crows, the murderous laughter of their cawing ringing in her ears.

Chapter 4

Ryan swiped blindly at the crows as they bit and flew at him. Through the heavy flicker of dark wings all about he caught the scene in flashes: the Doctor and Yaz were huddled together; Graham was spinning in a circle, flailing about; Alp lay prone and bloody as the storm of black feathers consumed him. Only Bleda seemed more or less unaffected, curled into a ball.

A rook landed on Ryan's chest, and its huge, sharp beak started hammering at his neck. Next second it was knocked clear by a hoof as Bittenmane jumped over Ryan, rearing up and kicking out at the storm of black around him. But the birds didn't seem interested in the horse; the rooks and ravens tore instead at the gruesome heads that hung and bounced from the leather strap about the horse's neck.

It's like the birds have been programmed to attack humans, Ryan realised numbly. *This isn't random. They were sent here. Targeted. Witchcraft.*

The idea cast a horrid spell on Ryan, robbing him of reason as ravens flew at him, clawing at his clothes, slicing at his back with curved scissor beaks. Desperate for cover, Ryan broke into a stumbling run, hoping to escape them. He tried to look at his feet, to place himself into the space about him as he crashed through twigs and bracken. He heard Graham shout, but the sound was growing fainter and Ryan's body felt heavy, his eyes were watering, he could barely see, and still the birds kept thundering down around him, *into* him. Ryan's head struck something hard – a tree trunk, maybe – and he fell, face-first into mud. He felt the birds writhing about him, biting at his neck, hammering at the backs of his hands as he tried to protect himself. He couldn't breathe, pain was knifing through his limbs—

A high-pitched hum shocked through Ryan's head. The pain felt physical in his brain. *Can't take that*, he thought, screwing his eyes shut. He wasn't sure how long it stayed dark but suddenly there was noise and movement at his ear, and something was carving a path through the feathered mass, helping him up. Ryan wiped at his eyes.

Graham's face – pale, scratched and concerned – was up in his own. 'It's OK, mate. Cuts and scrapes, but you'll be all right.'

'You came after me?'

'Course I did! Thought I'd lost you.' Graham leaned on Bleda's sword like a walking stick. 'You're definitely winning at the whole space-awareness thing, you took off like you had wings yourself.'

'That noise in my head.' Ryan tried to calm his breathing. 'Was that the sonic?'

'Must've been. Guess the Doc scrambled those birds' feathered brains long enough to break whatever was controlling them.'

'A witch's spell?' Ryan looked around the eerily lit forest. 'Guess we'd better get back.'

Graham nodded and they turned.

'Oh, my days,' said Ryan.

An old woman, her face sinister in shadow, was watching them from just a few metres away. She was dressed in sackcloth rags, and her narrowed eyes held a golden glow. 'Who are you?' Her voice sounded ancient, like two people speaking – one high and weary, the other unnaturally deep. 'What do you bring to our world?'

Graham swallowed hard, glanced at Ryan. 'Your world?'

Ryan backed him up. 'It's our world too, last time I checked.' He lowered his voice to Graham. 'Alp said the Huns' witch-woman was dead. This must be the Romans' one.'

'Right,' said Graham, before raising his voice: 'Um, *viva Roma*?'

'Who are you?' the old woman said again, unmoving in the shadow of a dead tree. A stench of decay carried with her words. 'The Tenctrama must know.'

A wolf came out from behind her rotting skirts, and then two more. She held out taloned fingers and all three beasts growled.

Graham and Ryan looked at each other for a moment's unspoken conference. Then, with a nod, they both turned and ran.

*

Defiant, the Doctor's arm was held up straight like a periscope, the sonic screwdriver clamped in her hand, its resonant whirr dying away under the heavy *kaah* and *kreee* of the carrion birds as they shuddered and fell.

Ears ringing and cuts stinging, Yaz scrambled to join the Doctor. 'Mass bird attack, what was that about?'

'No idea. If they'd been griffon vultures I could maybe understand, but …' She pushed herself up on her hands, blew the hair from her face. 'Sorry about the bad vibrations. That was an unkindness of ravens all right …' Her hair hung over her eyes as she sadly searched the ground. 'And a murder of crows.'

Yaz felt cold to find the clearing carpeted with large, black birds. 'They're dead? Did the sonic …?'

'I didn't kill them.' The Doctor was stroking a dead jackdaw, staring at it, distressed. 'Whatever controlled them did when it was done with them.' She placed the bird back down on the ground. 'Or … maybe they were already dead?'

'Zombie crows?' Yaz said, frowning.

'Will you witches never be silent?' Bleda was cradling Alp and stroking the man's bloodied lolling head. 'Alp's heart has stopped. He is dead.'

'Oh, no. I'm so sorry.' The Doctor crawled closer to see. 'He was already weak from losing so much blood, the shock of a further attack—'

'Alp was never weak.' Bleda's voice was a fierce hiss. 'Battle did not kill him, Tenctrama magicks did.' He paused, traced a finger over a particularly livid scar on Alp's cheek. 'While your magicks saved me.'

'Science, not magicks.'

'You can make other magicks?' He got to his feet. 'Magicks to help the Huns?'

'To be honest, it's my own tribe I'm more worried about right now.' The Doctor cupped her hands to her mouth. 'Ryan? Graham!'

'Where'd they go?' Yaz felt fear start to ball in her stomach. 'I couldn't see, my eyes were full of crows …'

'The force-field generator's gone too.' The Doctor crouched beside Bittenmane who lay on the forest floor, trembling but otherwise untouched. She stroked his flank, soothing him. 'Maybe Graham or Ryan picked it up?'

'Does it look like a long crystal tied with strips of metal?' asked Bleda.

'Pretty much!' The Doctor jumped up. 'Did you find it?'

'I did.' Bleda held the force-field generator in both hands, pointing it at the Doctor and Yaz. His smile was gloating. 'I wield your magicks now, witches.'

Chapter 5

Graham had his arm round Ryan to help steer and support the lad as the two of them legged it through the forest. Sweating hard and panting harder, he was grateful for the garish night-light the sky had become: it helped them pick a path through the trees.

And stopped them running straight into a charnel ground of dead soldiers.

'Oh my God …' Graham skidded to a halt, and Ryan almost overbalanced.

The dead men looked to be Huns, dressed like Bleda and his mate. They bore fresh, livid welts on their faces. 'The birds got them an' all,' Ryan said. 'Look.'

With a shiver, Graham saw that there were crows lying among the dead. One still had its huge grey beak buried in a man's windpipe. 'Could've been us,' he whispered, a hand straying to a cut on his own cheek.

Then he heard the familiar growl of wolves behind them. Graham and Ryan turned to find the snarling beasts gazing from the gloom with golden eyes. They could have caught up easily, Graham supposed; it was as if they'd been told to follow, to watch.

Then a sickly-sweet stink of putrefaction caught in his nostrils. Graham turned back to the glade of the dead – and he and Ryan gasped and clung together.

The Tenctrama witch-woman was back, hovering above the field of corpses like a spectre of death. Somehow she'd got ahead of them. And now the burning sky revealed her form in full.

Her skin was white as maggots, puckered and etched with deep lines. The features were loose approximations of human norms – the nose a bump with two flaring holes, the mouth a lopsided slit, cheekbones clinging to sunken eye sockets. The eyes themselves were fixed on him, irises sickly yellow with three pupils rolling in each; from the lower lid, lashes hung down like threadworms over the sallow skin. A thicket of grey hair framed the whole. Slowly she gestured to the pile of bodies.

'I've saved a place for you,' she hissed.

Yaz held perfectly still just beside Bleda. She remembered the way he'd been thrown across the clearing, propelled by the force-field generator when it had been held by someone who knew – near enough, at least – what they were doing. In his hands ...

'You don't understand, Bleda.' The Doctor slipped the sonic into her coat pocket and slowly crossed the clearing. 'You need to put down that crystal rod, there's a crack in the circuit, residual energy is building unpredictably—'

'You need to be silent, witch!' Bleda sneered. 'What you did to me, I shall learn to do to others.'

'Doctor!' Yaz's attention was caught by a golden glow at the edge of the dark, encroaching trees to her left. The apparition of a figure, gnarled and wizened, was rising up from the ground. 'Doctor, what is *that*?'

Bleda swung around to see, raising the generator. At the sudden movement it glowed sun-bright.

The Doctor sprinted for the cover of the TARDIS. 'Yaz, *get down—!*'

Yaz hit the deck just as a subsonic punch doubled her over, leaving her insides hollow. A belt of invisible energy tore from the force-field generator in Bleda's hands and the world was ripped away. The trees and the undergrowth were stripped away, blown on the air like dandelion clocks in a hurricane.

Yaz found herself flat beside Bleda on a tiny island of untouched mulch in a basin of dust, holding herself, gasping for breath. The space around for twenty metres was one of dead and twisted trees. The figure had vanished. The TARDIS had been knocked clean over, lying on its front, doors to the ground. Alp's body lay twisted a few metres away, and the Doctor …

She was nowhere to be seen.

Bleda stood untouched, staring at the cracked and blackened tube in his hand. 'Such magicks,' he breathed.

'What have you done?' Yaz looked up at Bleda. 'Where's the Doctor—'

'I'm all right! I'm all right.' The Doctor jumped up from behind the TARDIS and stood there, swaying, a dazed smile on her face. 'No one panic! I found cover in time. I'm fine! I'm super fine.'

She collapsed face-first over the police box.

Graham felt a pressure behind his ears, felt his senses distort and the world bend as if the hovering witch-woman was drawing him in with her searing eyes.

Then the long moment that locked them together ended as a tremor shook through the ground. Graham was thrown forward and Ryan with him as a storm of white energy went fireflying through the air.

The Tenctrama's old, hunched body bent over backwards, split apart as the golden light knifed out from inside her, cobwebbing up across the sky like a blazing beacon. Graham closed his eyes, and when he opened them again, the woman, and the light show, had disappeared, and the ashen light was fading. Natural darkness fell across the forest, a crescent moon pinned to its backcloth.

The sudden calm brought Graham no relief; when you've seen horrors in the light, you know that darkness only masks them. His eyes adjusted: while the witch-woman had truly gone, she'd left the lifeless bodies of three wolves behind – and the littering of dead Huns where they'd fallen.

'Well, that wasn't at all horrific.' Ryan got up and winced. 'Oh, my days, those birds did a number on me.'

Graham looked him over. 'You're lucky. A few scrapes and bruises. Not so bad.'

Both he and Ryan froze as a fresh crashing carried from the forest.

'Everyone out!' A man's bark, hoarse with fear; too close. 'Attila's worms aren't worth it and Queile has disappeared. There must be other hags loose in the forest. Out, now!'

'That's got to be Roman soldiers,' said Ryan, 'between us and the TARDIS.'

'We'll have to try circling round to find the Doctor and Yaz,' Graham said.

'While not getting killed by every single other thing in this stupid forest.'

'Not a bad plan.'

'Cheers.'

'I mean, you've had worse …'

Staying low to the ground in an awkward crouch, Graham and Ryan moved quickly away, skirting the forest's fringes.

As they departed, one of the fallen soldiers twitched dead muscles in his dead neck. Slowly lifted his dead head.

Watched them go, through dead eyes.

Chapter 6

Am I getting old or what?

Time was, thought the Doctor, the impact blast from a misfiring force-field generator would've given her nothing more than some colourful bruising and a dicky tummy, particularly so near the eye of the storm. But here and now …

No. This was not your typical slip into unconsciousness. The darkness about her was sentient somehow, pooling up from the ground. The force field had swept it clear for a time, like water from a tap washes blood from a wound. But the wound remained, and the darkness, like blood, was seeping back.

It was bitey, this darkness, and flecked with gold. Countless little golden teeth nibbling at her, golden needle-tongues poking through the tiny wounds to taste her, a billion shining sub-atomic admirers wanting in. The Doctor could feel the invisible glow building in the shattered glade; it tingled through the scorched soil, trembled through the dying roots of splintered trees, shining in the corpses of the million tiny insects already rotting in the mud depths.

I ought to wake up, thought the Doctor, as the glow built and beguiled her. *I really, really ought to rise and …*

Shine.

Trussed up and bundled onto a two-wheeled, horse-drawn cart, bumping along the roughest track in the world with Alp's corpse on one side and the sleeping Doctor on the other, Yaz fretted over her friends and wondered how much of this miserable night still remained.

Where were Graham and Ryan now? In her most hopeful daydreams, other Huns caught them and brought them back to Bleda's camp, so they would be reunited. In her worst imaginings, the sinister apparition she'd glimpsed before figured highly. The image of something old and twisted, an atmosphere of anger and malevolence …

Somehow she knew it hadn't gone for good. That she would be seeing it again.

Yaz looked down at the Doctor and found her smiling in her sleep, oblivious. With a pang of bitterness Yaz thought, *Wish I was.*

Bleda had led the way from the dead clearing in fine style: he'd stolen the sonic, swung the sleeping Doctor over his shoulder and held his curved dagger to her ribs, threatening a swift incision if Yaz didn't play barbarian ball. And so Yaz had been forced to lead Bittenmane meekly along by his reins with Alp's broken body slung across his back, through the remains of the shattered forest.

They'd chanced on the upturned cart still hitched to the terrified horses – abandoned after the animal attack or the force-field explosion, who could tell. Once they'd righted that, Bleda had bound her wrists with Alp's leather lasso and shoved her on the cart alongside her prostrate companions while he rode one of the two horses pulling them and Bittenmane trotted alongside. They were following Attila's retreating Huns, a trail that was hard to miss since the muddy track had been churned all to hell, and the cart creaked and rocked from side to side, throwing Yaz around until her bruises had bruises. Bleda just glanced back at her now and then, smiling like a hunter who knew he was bringing back one hell of a meal to put on the table.

For all he was a hairy maniac, Bleda had played things pretty shrewdly. There were no signs of any Romans left in the area now: most likely they'd been scared to death by the force-field eruption and all legged it back to camp. The glow had gone from the night, too, so presumably the hunt for Huns was over.

Bleda gave a short, sharp whistle to his horses and they slowed and veered left towards some scrubby plants. Bittenmane began to crop the choicest greenery and the other two horses ate around him, straining against their reins.

It was Bleda's feeding time too, it seemed. He reached behind him, pulled something wormy and grey from under his horse's saddle and stuffed it into his mouth.

Yaz stared. 'What did you just eat?'

'Meat.'

'Meat that's been left on a horse's back under a saddle?'

'Want some?'

'Is it halal?'

'What?'

'Think I'll leave it, thanks.'

He scoffed. 'You can magick us a ten-course feast, if you wish.'

'Only I can't.' Yaz was losing patience. 'Because, like I keep telling you, I'm not magic. The force-field generator isn't magic. It's just a special kind of tool that was damaged when we—'

'Yasmin,' said Bleda, thoughtfully, 'you are a very boring witch. Be happy, like your Doctor. See, she smiles! She knows her wand did good magicks, knocking down the forest. Better magicks than the Tenctrama.'

'For the last time, it's science that knocked down the forest!'

'Then science is also magick. Who cares?' He shrugged his big shoulders. 'It is for scribes to know the difference.'

Yaz shook her head, wearily. 'If scribes really do know the difference, please can we see a scribe?'

'No.' Bleda swallowed his meat and his crafty smile returned. 'But I will show you great Attila.'

Yaz felt her prickling palms turn clammy. Meeting with Attila the Hun! The idea of being surrounded by thousands of warriors like Bleda, an unstoppable, nightmare force as scary as any aliens, trampling reason and civilisation under their hairy, smelly feet ...

'Here.' Bleda rooted again beneath the saddle for some more grey gristle and held it out to her. 'Even a boring witch should eat.'

Set to feed him a piece of her mind, Yaz opened her mouth – as the Doctor's peaceful smile exploded into a scream, and she sat bolt upright, shaking and panting for breath.

'Doctor!' Yaz tried to put an arm around her and winced. Her wrists were still tied tight, of course. 'Easy, Doctor, it's all right …'

'No.' The Doctor's eyes were wide and watery, she looked traumatised. 'No, I don't think it is all right. No. It's really not.' She looked around wildly in the darkness, struggling to free her hands from behind her back. 'Oh. Bleda's taken us prisoner?'

Bleda watched the Doctor beadily. 'You belong to the Huns now.'

'The sonic. Where's my sonic?'

'Your magick rods also belong to the Huns.'

'Well, that's a comfort. I always wanted the best for them.'

As Bleda whistled to the horses and they set the cart moving again, the Doctor took deep breaths and puffed them back out. 'What about Graham and Ryan – do *they* belong to the Huns?'

'The rooks and ravens chased your slaves into the forest, remember?'

'They're not slaves, they're our friends.' Yaz rested her head against the Doctor's. 'Bleda wouldn't let me look for them.'

'If we found them, you would outnumber me four to one!' Bleda scoffed. 'Do not fear, witches. Attila will give you better slaves than them if you serve him loyally.'

Yasmin shook her head. 'He thinks we're witches. Well, you're the full-on witch, and I'm magic too.'

'Course you are. I thought you looked *familiar*.' The Doctor grinned. 'As in witch's familiar. Yeah?'

Yaz forced a smile for her friend's benefit. 'Look, here's my familiar grin.'

'Then things aren't all bad.' The Doctor grew serious. 'With any luck, Graham and Ryan will get back to the TARDIS. They should be safe there.' She looked down at Alp's lifeless body beside her. 'This is a dangerous world.'

'Where did *you* go to, Doctor?' Yaz asked. 'You were out cold for ages, but you were … smiling.'

'Was I?' The Doctor pulled a variety of manic and slightly disturbing grins. 'Like this?'

'No, sort of peaceful.'

'Peaceful? I was having a nightmare. I couldn't leave the clearing. Something wanted me to stay there till it was ready …' She frowned. 'No. Until *I* was ready.'

Yaz frowned. 'Ready for what?'

'I don't know. But I'll tell you what – I'm starving.'

'Then eat, Witch-Doctor!' Bleda pushed his hand under the saddle for a further scrap of grey meat, and offered it behind him to the Doctor, who leaned forward and took it in her teeth.

Yaz grimaced. 'You're not actually …!'

But she was, she was chewing it. 'Not bad! And very practical.' The Doctor licked her lips. 'See, the meat is warmed by the horse's flesh and tenderised by the pressure of the saddle. And because it's salted, it doesn't go off. It's preserved …' As the cart jerked away, she looked down at Alp's body. 'You know how salt preserves things? Basically osmosis. Salt draws moisture out of organic cells, drying the meat and destroying the mould and microbes that want to destroy it. Use enough salt, you can preserve meat for months. Years, even. Nice, well-stocked larder.'

'It would be totally gross to eat, though,' said Yaz.

'Someone might have a different use for that super-salted meat than just eating it.' The Doctor didn't look up. 'Like, left outside in your garden, all that salt could kill the local slugs.'

'I hate slugs.' Yaz stared at her. 'Doctor, what are you on about?'

With a sudden rush of breath, Alp opened his dead, grey eyes. Yaz cried out in surprise, which made Bleda start. He looked back, and his black eyes widened. Alp sat stiffly, his arms twitching, hands clenching and unclenching, mouth hanging dry, dark and open.

'He lives,' hissed Bleda. 'This is your work, Doctor?'

The Doctor shook her head; she wasn't afraid, she just looked thoughtful. 'Just spitballing here … but do you think that creatures from far away who were clever with salt could tell much difference between us and the slugs?'

Chapter 7

The night was long and the going was hard and the fields went on for ever and ever, apparently. Ryan was tired of following Graham's backside through the undergrowth, but accepted the need for caution. Didn't matter if Huns or Roman soldiers spotted them; both sides would happily use them for sword practice. And as for running into any more witches, well, no way was that on his bucket list …

What Ryan didn't accept was that they weren't completely lost.

They'd had to make a couple of detours. The Romans were using one side of the forest as an assembly point for troops, returning from bloody skirmishes with the Huns, and attempts to circle round them had been complicated by the course of a river – a river that was a magnet for thirsty soldiers, wounded soldiers and any other soldier caught short, to say nothing of their various horses. So, basically, don't drink the water and stay well away. But as a result, in the dark, after all the stops and starts and retracing of steps, Ryan wasn't sure they were anywhere near to the forest where they'd find the TARDIS, Yaz and the Doctor.

'They'll wait for us,' Graham said, as if reading his mind.

Ryan stopped for a moment, leaned heavily against a tree. 'Yeah. They'll put themselves in danger waiting for us, and it's my fault. I should never have run.'

'You should never have become a piñata for a bunch of bleedin' birds, either, but it happened.'

For the tenth time, Ryan checked his phone: the display showed real-world, normal-day-in-Sheffield time, three minutes after noon – funnily enough Roman Gaul fifteen hundred years ago wasn't one of the pre-set time zones.

'Seriously, how many times have you pulled out that phone?'

'I'm looking at the time.'

'What is it, about X past V in the morning?'

'Ha, ha. Just wanted to know how long we've been going.' Ryan sighed and put the phone away. 'Nearly four hours.'

'IV hours, you mean. Best get moving. Watch your step this way. Steep hill, and the ground's uneven.'

'Then you'd best stand still, where you are.' The sonorous voice from behind them made both men jump and turn.

Two sinister figures sat astride jet-black horses. They wore scaled armour and helmets that hid their faces, more like medieval knights than your typical Roman cavalry. The horses had eye-guards and chain mail hung down from the saddles. A sword and a short lance were strapped to each rider's side. One of the horsemen edged his mount closer.

'Surrender,' came the deep voice again. 'You are prisoners of the Legion of Smoke.'

'Legion of Smoke,' Graham echoed. 'Right. Not at all creepy.'

We're not prisoners yet, thought Ryan. He still had his phone in his hand, and swiped his thumb upward over the screen. 'Get ready,' he whispered to Graham.

'Put up your hands,' said the horseman.

'OK,' said Ryan. He subtly tapped his thumb against the screen but nothing happened. *Yeah, turn on Bluetooth, that's gonna scare the Legion of Smoke.* Finally he connected with the right button.

And as his hand came fully up, the flashlight in his phone switched on, blinding bright. The horses shied, their riders put hands up to their faces. Ryan felt jubilant – they must be terrified!

'Vitus, their talk-box comes with a light in it!' the lead rider shouted. 'Get them!'

'Come on!' Graham grabbed Ryan by the arm and dragged him away. Ryan tried to hold the phone out behind him, to keep them blinded, until in a literal flash he realised he was also giving them the biggest possible trail to follow. The gallop of hoofbeats sounded close behind already. Ryan tried to turn off the torchlight, stumbled, the extremes of light and dark making it hard to stay balanced—

—and so he didn't. His left foot twisted under him on uneven ground, and Ryan pitched over the edge of the steep hill. He gasped as he hit the ground on his side, shoulder first, and went barrel rolling down the slope over the loose mud and scree. Winded, he came to a stop at the bottom of the hill, rolled into a tangle of vegetation and waited, heart thrumming, listening for sounds of pursuit.

Hold tight, he told himself. *Graham will see you've gone and double back. He'll be here any minute and the two of you can get going.*

As the moon raised its head from the churning clouds, Ryan saw a dark, armoured figure on horseback pick a path down the slope, heading straight for him.

'Ryan?' Graham felt sick as he continued his mad scramble through the woods. *I've lost him.* He imagined the look on Grace's face if she were here, if she knew. *I lost him, love, fifteen hundred years before he was ever born.* 'Ryan, mate, where are you?'

He couldn't hear anything but the crash and thump of hoofbeats behind and breaking branches all around. The soldier – Vitus, he'd been called – was charging along right behind him. Graham's chest was aching as much as his legs, and his mouth was dry. *Lead this bloke into the thicker parts of the forest*, he thought, *so he has to get off his horse. He's wearing armour, he might not be able to move as fast as you …*

Yeah, fastest granddad in the west, Graham thought dismally. *I've got to double back and help Ryan …*

There was a tangle of branches to his right off the path, and he ducked under it. To his dismay it gave onto a blackened clearing. A fire had been started in the middle of the space, a defensive strategy perhaps. Four corpses in clothes like Alp's and Bleda's lay around it. Hun bodies.

Bodies that began to twitch and twist, even as he looked at them.

It was a nightmarish sight: heads lolling on broken necks that somehow turned anyway, dead-jelly eyes fixing on him. Red-raw faces staring, all expression burned away, limbs cracking like dead branches as they began to rise. A thick goo like melting plastic started welling out from cracks in the crackling skin. The eyes were growing darker, misshapen lids blinking stiffly.

Horrified, Graham turned to run back the same way he'd come – just as Vitus burst through the thicket on horseback.

'It's really no use running!' the knight told him. 'Where can you go?'

Anywhere but here, thought Graham, glancing back in horror at the dead Huns rising. Talk about caught between a rock and a hard place! Except when the Doctor landed you in it, the rock had red eyes that fired laser beams and the hard place was probably sentient and set to swallow you up in one gulp.

At the sight of the knight, the four Hun zombies drew their swords. Vitus pulled up tensely on his horse's reins, and turned to Graham, who knew what expression lay behind that helmet. 'Allies of yours?'

'We've never met,' Graham said quickly.

One of the Huns spoke slowly: 'The Pit,' he said. 'All in the Pit …'

'Together in the Great Pit,' intoned another, and the two others began paraphrasing in an eerie mantra: 'All in the Pit … the Great Pit …'

There was a dirty great pit in the nearest Hun's charcoaled chest, Graham noted. But even as he watched, the wound healed over: raw, pale flesh spilling out from the cavity like blancmange to seal it in an enormous, clumsy patch. The burned faces too were sprouting new skin.

'What manner of creatures are you?' Vitus demanded, apparently trying to stare down the ghouls. 'I don't believe you are shades of the dead come back to haunt this Earth.'

Graham, on the other hand, was prepared to give them the benefit of the doubt. He was going to suggest that both he and Vitus run for it, when he realised the Hun-creatures had their attention pegged purely on the Roman. Wielding their soot-caked swords they advanced on Vitus, still muttering the same words over and over: 'All fall … into the Pit … the Great Pit takes us …'

Vitus swung himself down from his horse and raised his own sword in warning. It soon became clear that his opponents were no lumbering, brainless zombies. There was a jerk and a twitch to their movements, but they attacked with horrible speed. As they parried and struck at their Roman enemy, Graham was put in mind of murderous stop-motion monsters from a Harryhausen movie. Only these things were real, and driving Vitus back from the clearing, their murmurings drowned out by the ring and clash of steel on steel.

'Run for it, then!' Graham yelled at Vitus. Then he tore his eyes away from the nightmare battle and followed his own advice.

Chapter 8

Scarcely protected by his tangle of bracken, Ryan watched as the dark rider brought his mount to a halt at the bottom of the hill in the moon's six-watt spotlight. Then the helmeted figure swung nimbly to the ground.

'I see you there,' came the voice from behind the helmet, metallic and resonant.

Ryan held still; this guy could be bluffing.

'I see you there, lying down in that undergrowth.' The voice sounded almost amused. 'Come out and face me.'

All right, thought Ryan, *he's not bluffing. So maybe it's time I had a go.* He turned on his phone, got up slowly and pulled up the World of Combat app. He'd last been playing as a Spartan foot-soldier, and his fearsome-looking avatar filled the screen, waving its thick, curved iron sword and a circular, patterned shield. Ryan took a deep breath, and stepped out through the undergrowth, holding the screen towards the sinister figure. The dark rider stepped back and drew his sword.

'See this?' Ryan thrust the phone out. 'It's a … magic prison, right? Full of magic warriors! Magic warriors who will fight for me.'

'Is that a Spartan foot-soldier? Fascinating.' The legionary tilted his head to one side, staring at the screen. 'Such colour and detail. Like no combat magicks I have seen.'

'And you don't want to see it, trust me,' Ryan said. 'My granddad – my fellow warrior, I mean – he's got magic too. Your mate does not want to mess with him.'

'Can you make the bright light come on again?'

'I can, but I won't, for your sake. Second time, it would … really hurt your eyes. Now, go! Before I let out this guy and he kicks off.'

The legionary straightened up. 'Very well. Let him out.'

'Er …'

'Please? I'd like to observe how a large soldier emerges from such a small space. It's bigger on the inside, perhaps.'

Ryan cleared his throat. 'Well, that would be stupid.'

'Like the clay jar that Pandora opened, letting demons out into the world.'

'Jar? I thought it was Pandora's box?'

'It was a jar. Everyone knows it was a jar.' The legionary crossed his arms. 'Come on, then. Out with your Spartan warrior.'

Ryan shifted uncomfortably. 'I'm going to give you one more chance to run.'

'You can't do it, can you?' The voice had grown lighter, higher in pitch, and actually sounded disappointed. 'What is that device, really? Vitus saw you with it and thought it might be a talk-box. But it has a light in it, too, and moving pictures of Spartans. What sort of a tool does all this?' The legionary sighed as Ryan stayed silent. 'Do you not know how it works? Did it fall from the sky, perhaps, and you caught it?'

'I … don't know what you're on about.'

'Oh, come off it!' The legionary removed his helmet – but it wasn't a bloke after all. A woman's face looked back at him: mid-twenties, black-haired with wide grey eyes and cheekbones you could shave with. 'Look, we were both trying to fool each other. How about now we take a minute to be honest?'

'All right.' Slowly, Ryan lowered his phone. 'Who are you?'

'My name's Licinia Postuma. Yours?'

'Ryan Sinclair.'

'Weird name.'

'Least I'm not pretending to be something I'm not.'

'I've learned that very little in this world is as it seems. Why should I be?' Licinia sheathed her sword. 'Truth is, it helps with interrogation. I bring them in as a man, then put myself in the next cell as little Licinia.' She sighed. 'People seem to talk faster and freer to a female fellow prisoner.'

'There aren't many of you in the Legion of Smoke, then?' Ryan noted that she didn't answer; perhaps she didn't want to be *too* honest. 'How about Vitus, is he a girl too, or …?'

'He's a man.' Licinia looked him hard in the eye. 'What kind of a man are you, Ryan? Now I've seen you clearly, you're no Hun.'

'How'd you know?'

'A fighting people are proud of their wounds: to a Hun, the more scars on a man's face, the more handsome it is. That's why Huns don't flinch from injury in battle.' Licinia shrugged. 'You've got a few fresh scratches. So either you're a prince or a general, kept safe by bodyguards – or else you're the ugliest Hun who's ever lived.'

'Oh.' Ryan blinked. 'Cheers.'

'And I don't believe you're ugly. I believe you are from a strange and far-off province.' A pause and a smile. 'And handsome.'

'Right. Well …'

'Which is it?'

'I'm handsome, from Britannia.'

'Britannia has strange tailors.'

'I guess.' Ryan looked down at his jeans and hoodie and gave her a bashful grin. 'You seem pretty chilled about everything.'

'I keep my mind open and consider the evidence,' she said.

'Like this.' Ryan looked ruefully at his phone. 'I thought this would impress you.'

'Not as a weapon. What is it really for?'

'You were right, it *is* a talk-box.'

Licinia looked suddenly childlike in her excitement. 'Like mine?' She pulled out a small slab of metal, a little smaller than his mobile, and put it to her ear. 'Vitus, can you hear me?' The metal glowed blue, and she waved it at Ryan. 'Light! Like yours.'

Ryan smiled. 'Mine's brighter.'

'Than its owner? So I've observed.' Licinia spoke into her communicator again. 'Vitus?' There was no response.

'Trouble, you think?'

'The talk-boxes were found centuries ago in strange wreckage. They don't always work perfectly. Perhaps that's it.' She looked at Ryan. 'I hope your "fellow warrior" hasn't hurt him.'

'Graham? Ha! When I said that, I meant, "fellow *worrier*",' said Ryan. 'Mostly we worry about Huns, wolves, the Tenctrama …'

'What?' Immediately Licinia's face grew harder. 'What do you know about the Tenctrama?'

'The Romans killed one called Enkalo who was helping the Huns.'

'*Killed* her?' Now Licinia was like a dog with ears pricked up having just heard 'Walkies'. She started bouncing with excitement, her armour rattling. 'Killed how? What happened?'

'I dunno, exactly.'

'What about the Romans' witch, Queile? Have you seen her? Vitus and I were out looking for her when we found you with your talk-box.'

'I saw one of the witches explode in light—'

'You actually saw a Tenctrama die?' She grabbed him by his T-shirt. 'What happened?'

He tried to pull free. 'She just disappeared in a big lightshow.'

'This light, was there any physical trace afterwards, any damage to the surrounding environment? Any ectoplasm?'

'Ecto-what now?'

'Discharge?'

'Ewww!'

'Well?'

'I dunno, didn't stick around to find out!'

Licinia groaned with frustration. 'OK. We'll take things slowly. We'll go over all you know. Full interrogation.'

Ryan frowned. 'What?'

'Figure of speech. But we're too exposed out here. Come on, I'll take you to the Depot.'

'Depot?'

'Local base of operations.' She patted her mount on the back and made a stirrup with her hands. 'Quickly! Climb on board.'

'Um, I can't,' Ryan said quickly. 'I'll fall straight off.'

'So, be careful.'

'You don't get it. I have a bit of a problem with balance.' He paused, recalled the well-worn words his doctor used to say, licked his lips. 'There's a difference between how well I *could* do something, and how well I actually do it.'

Licinia raised an eyebrow. 'If only all men were as honest as you, Ryan, I might not be as bitterly disappointed as I've turned out.' She smiled. 'I won't make you ride Reduxa. Just sit on her while I lead you to our offices. For all we know, Vitus is bringing your friend Graham there right now.'

Ryan's heart made an optimistic lurch: *Maybe I can do this?* Clumsily, concentrating hard, he accepted Licinia's bunk-up and, after three goes, wound up clinging on to the horse's broad back for dear life.

'Well,' he said, through gritted teeth. 'What are we waiting for?'

'For you to wear this.' Licinia held up a small black sack. 'Sorry, but the Legion of Smoke operates in utter secrecy.'

Ryan sighed, optimism standing down. 'What even *is* the Legion of Smoke?'

'Understaffed. Underfunded. Under orders to explain the inexplicable. Lucky for you we're not too far away, so you'll soon see.' She smiled in apology. 'Well, you'll see when we get there.'

She pulled the sack down over Ryan's face.

Chapter 9

'Are we nearly there?'

Yaz knew she sounded like a bored teen in the back seat of the car, but inside she felt more like a child cowering under the covers. This endless journey in the cart had got a hundred times worse and weirder since Alp had snapped back from the dead. He was sitting up in the wagon propped up on his big bruised hands, muttering under his breath. The Doctor had asked Bleda to untie her hands so she might examine him properly, but the Hun had refused. So instead, she had passed the journey through the dark hunched over in unlikely positions, pressing her ear to his chest, taking his pulse, checking his reflexes.

'I said, are we nearly there?' Yaz tried again.

'We approach the plains, where our camp stands.' Bleda sounded tired. 'Alp. Alp, I said, we are near the camp. Are you awake?'

Alp was awake all right, his eyes unblinking, flicking all about, muttering something about pits.

'The lights are on,' said the Doctor, sitting up straight and clicking her neck. 'But I'm not sure who's home.'

'He is strong, Alp,' Bleda said, ignoring her. 'I thought he was dead, but he was only sleeping deeply.'

'Deeper than you think.' The Doctor leaned in to Yaz. 'There's no heartbeat. Not a pulse to be had anywhere.'

'So what's done this to him?' asked Yaz. 'The Tenctrama?'

'That's my guess. All part of the combat magicks. Soldiers who can't die. It's a general's dream. They can't even be hurt, there's no response to stimulus.' She lowered her voice. 'Not even when I prodded his leg with the point of his own dagger.'

Yaz raised her eyebrows. 'You've got his dagger?' Even as she spoke, she felt the tug at her wrists as the blade chewed against the leather cord. The Doctor grinned and mouthed at her to hold still. Yaz looked worriedly at Alp – would he try to stop them, raise the alarm? No, he was staring away from them, past the stumps of felled trees that lined the churned-up track, out into the night.

'Let's keep our driver distracted.' The Doctor raised her voice. 'Tell me, Bleda. Tell me about Attila. I reckon you must know him pretty well.'

Bleda glanced back, his smile cold and haughty. 'I've known him all my life.'

'So tell me, why do your people have so much faith in him?'

'Because Attila is invincible.'

'Never much cared for the word "invincible". Quite smug, isn't it?' The Doctor turned up her nose. 'The opposite of "invincible" is "vincible", Yaz, but who says that any more? If you think about it, in a way, *vincible* was conquered by *invincible*, and now *invincible* endures.

Invincibly! See? It's like nominative determinism for words.'

Bleda snorted as the cart shuddered noisily over a pothole. 'You are a very annoying witch.'

'Probably!' The Doctor frowned suddenly. 'Attila, though. He's got a dozen different peoples behind him, fighting in his army as if they're Huns themselves. Doesn't his needing the Tenctrama smack of *vincibility* in the eyes of the world?'

'Attila allows them to serve. Inkri, their wisest and eldest, came to his father, Mundzuk, many years ago. She explained that the Tenctrama had warred among themselves and broken into factions. Each group went to different territories and approached different rulers, seeking to trade their magicks in return for protection. But Inkri knew that Mundzuk's son, Attila, was destined to rule all – and so she and her sister, Enkalo, swore to make the Huns stronger than all other nations, to make us—'

'Invincible?' The Doctor nodded. 'I imagine the other Tenctrama said the same to your rivals.'

'It makes no difference, for Attila is stronger than them all!' Bleda swore. 'Accepting aid from the Tenctrama was good for all Huns. The Tenctrama have helped us. Grown special herbs that make us faster, stronger … bred beasts that will fight for us … provided crops that thrive on stony ground against all nature to feed our multitudes …'

'But if each side has the same advantages, then each side has none,' the Doctor concluded. 'Makes you wonder what they fell out about in the first place, doesn't it? If they're all after the same thing.'

'It doesn't matter,' Bleda growled. 'Attila now has an advantage the others don't: the two of you, and your different magicks. Stronger magicks.'

'Oh! You're recruiting for the post of Magical Adviser to Attila the Hun!' The Doctor's eyes locked with Yaz's. 'What a good job we're *free* to apply.'

Finally, Yaz felt the last strand of leather snap and could've cried with relief as she flexed and shook her wrists. Then a terrible smell made her eyes water in quite another way. 'Ugh, what's that?'

The Doctor pretended to roll the smell around her mouth. 'I'm getting pitch, smoke and excrement. And sore nostrils.'

'We are nearing the camp,' Bleda announced. 'Be quiet. The approach may be dangerous. Rome will have spies and scouts in the area, keeping eyes on our actions.' He whistled to the horses, who stopped abruptly, Bittenmane too. 'There they are, you see? The plains of Catalaunum.'

'Scenic stop!' hissed the Doctor. 'Love it!'

'The chosen battleground.'

'Chosen by Attila?' asked the Doctor. 'Or by the Tenctrama?'

Bleda declined to answer, which Yaz took to mean the latter. In the pinkening light of dawn, Yaz could see that they were halfway down a rolling hill that bordered an enormous and near-featureless plain. 'It goes on for miles and miles,' she breathed, eyes adjusting, slowly making sense of the details. A river flowed at the borders and a long, high ridge rose in the distance. Nestling perhaps a mile away was a town with low, conical buildings made of stone with tall, thatched roofs; it was like a reconstruction that *Blue Peter* presenters might visit but, no, this was the real deal, an archaeologist's dream standing before her.

Beyond the town was the camp. She could only see the shadow of it in the weak light, but there were sounds too along with the stink: the ring as hammers struck anvils, the clank and clatter of heavy lifting, and voices raised in what might have been prayer, or laments. Far away across the plain, the shadows seethed with movement. She saw with a chill that men and wagons, thousands and thousands of them, were moving in a column like ants.

'Something is wrong.' Bleda seemed concerned. 'I had ordered that our allies the Gepids were to be stationed at the River Aube, to cover our armies and force the Romans to come at us from the west, so they would fight with the morning sun in their eyes.'

The Doctor looked at Bleda. 'So you're Commander of the Ten Thousand Horsemen *and* Gepids Monitor? That's a lot of responsibility.'

The Hun did not reply, but he seemed deeply troubled.

'Well, I'm no expert,' the Doctor told him, 'but it looks to me like the Romans have broken through your lines. They'll be facing you from the east when battle comes.'

As she spoke, four black horses erupted from the bracken lining the track to block the way ahead.

These were no short, hairy Hun horses like Bittenmane. To Yaz, they looked like police horses from back home. Each stood perhaps fifteen hands high, powerful and muscular with arched necks and high-set tails.

'Where'd they come from?' Yaz wondered aloud.

The hedgerows were suddenly alive with fists and swords as half a dozen Roman legionaries burst out from either side of the track.

'Ambush!' roared Bleda.

Alp snapped into action, leaping down from the cart. Fearless and unarmed, he grabbed one of the legionaries by the throat and started to squeeze.

On instinct, Yaz flattened herself down inside the rocking cart beside the Doctor as the violence exploded around them. She heard Bleda dismount, swearing and threatening; the swoop and swing and clash of swords. Risking a look, Yaz saw Alp smash his victim to the ground. Another legionary stabbed Alp in the back with his sword, but the Hun noticed nothing; he swung round, gripped the man's head and shoulder and snapped his neck.

'Keep down,' the Doctor told Yaz. 'I've got to get the sonic.' She vaulted over the side of the cart.

'Doctor, wait!' Yaz sat up automatically, saw the Doctor duck under a swinging sword and heard Roman voices rise over the holler of battle.

'That's not possible,' shouted one of the Romans. 'He's up and fighting.'

'It cannot be,' another whimpered. 'Macro was dead. Throat slit! *Macro was dead!*'

A man loomed up over Yaz, his skin black and shiny, his features locked in hatred, his throat a gory beard of dried, blackened blood; Macro, she presumed. He raised a short and bloody sword, ready to drive it down into Yaz's chest.

Chapter 10

Graham forced a path through the tangled trees, trying to double back round to where he'd lost Ryan. He felt sick with fear and worry. What had happened to the lad? Was Vitus still alive? Who was his friend? Where were Yaz and the Doc now?

For that matter, where the hell was he?

He wandered around, listening for sounds of battle or pursuit, but could hear only the blood-beat in his temples and the snatching of his breath. Finally he chanced upon the hill where the spooky knights had shown up, and followed the horseshoe prints that ran down it. The clearing was empty, but here and there in the dirt he could see tracks. More horseshoes and— what was that?

He crouched down, muttering a prayer of thanks as he found the precise geometric imprint left behind by the soles of Ryan's sneakers, and some that were deeper and smeared. They vanished after that, but the hoofprints went on.

'Where's Bear Grylls when you need him?' Graham muttered as he set off, searching out the tracks.

Yaz felt her heart pound as if trying to bail from her chest before the murderous Macro could skewer it. She lifted both legs and kicked the man backwards. He fell staggering into Bittenmane, who reared up and knocked him down.

'Quick!' The Doctor was dancing towards Bleda through the thick of the fighting, dodging blows and blades. 'My sonic – the wand I used to stop the birds – gimme!'

Bleda punched aside a Roman and swung himself into Bittenmane's saddle. As he did so, he tossed the sonic at the Doctor, who caught it left-handed. She ducked as a sword swished over her head and jammed the sonic's tip against it. Electric crackles engulfed the sword and its owner dropped it, reeling backwards. But two more Romans were coming up from behind.

'Doctor, look out!' Yaz jumped from the cart onto the back of one, and his legs buckled so that he fell face down in the dirt. Then she pulled off the man's helmet and clobbered him with it. The Doctor turned, called 'Thank you!', then banged the sonic against the other Roman's breastplate. Sparks shot through the metal and with a high-pitched cry the man was sent somersaulting into a dazed heap beside the cart.

Yaz looked about to see how the fight was going, and wished she hadn't. One of the poor carthorses lay dead beside her, its companion straining to bolt with the cart but hitched to the dead weight. Alp was impaled on the end of a Roman sword, but he made no sound. He simply brought his hand down to snap the blade in two, twisted the jagged sword-stump from his would-be-killer's hand and thrust it into the man's chest. Then he reached behind him, took hold of the protruding blade by the gory point, and hurled it at the last Roman standing. A split second later, the sword-shaft was wedged in the man's torso, and he stood no more. Yaz stared with horrified fascination as the wound left in Alp's back bubbled with a clear fluid as if filling with hot fat, and soon healed over. All that was left was a scarlet scar.

You can't get stuff like that over the counter on Titan, she thought.

Where was Bleda? She saw him, still astride Bittenmane, fighting the undead Macro with his sword.

'This man won't fall!' Bleda snarled. For every stripe gouged in the man's flesh, the sizzling goo roiled up in place of blood to seal the wound. 'He's like Alp. This is Tenctrama work!'

Alp was ignoring his friend and comrade. He towered over Yaz, his face a pantomime grimace of hate, and with a thrust of his dagger killed the Roman she'd knocked out.

'No!' she shouted. 'That man was no threat to you!' But already Alp was turning murderously to the sonicked soldier down by the cart who was starting to stir.

The Doctor grabbed hold of Alp's sword arm, holding him back. 'No way, Alp, you've done enough,' she gasped. 'Help me, Yaz!'

Yaz got up and together they delayed Alp long enough for the dizzy legionary to register the danger he was in, roll over and stagger off in the opposite direction. As he fled from sight around the corner, Alp stopped struggling and stared down at the ground, suddenly oblivious to everything around him once more – including Bleda's ongoing struggle with Macro.

'All in the Pit,' Alp muttered. 'All of us join together in the Pit, all of us …'

'How about that. He'll kill a Roman who's hurting no one, but won't stop a zombie from trying to kill his commander.' The Doctor marvelled at the Hun. 'Looks like his bloodlust's reserved for the living, not the dead. Or us.'

Yaz shivered. 'Perhaps he wants Bleda to become like him?'

'Or perhaps he's been programmed with targets and we don't fit the brief,' said the Doctor. 'Another weapon handed over to both sides, to make the fighting worse.'

'Damn it, Alp!' Bleda turned to his countryman in fury. 'Would you let your king die in front of you and do nothing?'

Yaz raised her eyebrows. 'His *king*?'

Just then another dozen Huns came pushing through the hedgerows and, without hesitation, six or eight of them fell upon Macro, wrestling him to the ground. Yaz shut her eyes but she couldn't block the sickening sound of the swords as the Huns set about him. It was a long time before he fell silent.

Bleda swung himself down from Bittenmane, and the other Huns knelt before him.

'Attila lives!' the cry went up.

'Great Attila,' gushed one of the Huns. 'Praise the maker, you have returned to us.'

'But that's Bleda …' Yaz broke off. 'Oh. Oh, now, hang on …

The Doctor nodded. 'He's been playing us since we first met.'

Yaz looked at her. '*He's* Attila the Hun?' She groaned. 'That's why he made a big thing about being Bleda of the million horsemen when Alp came along. So the big guy didn't give the game away.'

'Watch these women carefully.' Attila's smile was regal as he signalled his men to close in on the Doctor and Yaz. 'They will not hurt you – they reject violence – but they're magical and devious.' He held out his hand. 'Return to me your wand, Doctor.'

'Can't,' said the Doctor. 'You fibbed to us. I don't reward fibbers.'

'You will die if you don't. No! Wait.' Attila smiled as he reconsidered. Slowly he crossed to Bittenmane and held a dagger to the chestnut neck. 'Do it, or the *horse* will die.'

Yaz felt sick. 'Bittenmane's yours. You wouldn't.'

'I have four hundred thousand like him in my camp. Well?'

'Well played, Attila. Very good.' Grudgingly, the Doctor handed the sonic to the nearest guard, who took it gingerly and passed it to Attila. 'So tell us. Who's Bleda?'

'Bleda is the name of my dead brother.'

'I'm sorry for your loss.'

'I'm not sorry I killed him.' Attila put the sonic away inside his tunic. 'You will excuse my deception, I trust?

Since my entire division was isolated from my retreating army by the magicks of the Roman Alliance, Aetius's curs have been searching from here to Orléans for the Lion of the Huns. I am hardly likely to announce my true identity to slaves and strangers.' He turned back to his men, who cowered from the anger in his eyes. 'And now, you, my people! You did not come to aid your king? You did not raze the forests to find me, did not throw yourselves upon my enemies to hasten my return?'

'My king …' One of the men, a noble like Alp from the looks of his finer clothes and the bling on his scabbard, stepped forward. 'Our troops have been searching for you in their thousands. Inkri the witch said she saw where you were in her dreams, she guided our raiding parties. But time and again, you had moved on and we found only the Roman legions or their allies waiting for us.'

Outrage twisted Attila's features. 'Inkri deceived you?'

'She claims Aetius's witches foretold our coming.' The noble shrugged, looking fearful. 'Our forces clashed. Hundreds died on both sides but we were no nearer finding you.'

'This reeks of witches' trickery …' Attila spat on the ground. 'And what of the Romans breaking our defences to strike from the east. Did the hags make that happen too?'

'There is much that has happened, Attila.' The noble looked grimly at Alp. 'Much we must show you.'

'Then do so.' Attila swung himself up onto Bittenmane. 'Come.'

Yaz looked at the Doctor as the guards shepherded them along the path down to the Hun encampment after Attila. 'Why would this Inkri trick the Huns now if she's been working for them for years? What game are the Tenctrama playing?'

'That's for them to know, and us to find out.' The Doctor looked at the mumbling Alp and the Roman remains on the track with stone cold eyes. 'And we find out now. There's been enough deaths chalked up to Tenctrama magic around here. One way or another, we bring an end to this today.'

Chapter 11

Ryan was feeling nauseated, lurching ever forward, arms clamped around Reduxa's neck, unable to see or even hear clearly, hot and half-suffocated by the sack over his head. 'Is it much further?'

'I've told you, no, it's not.' Licinia had, apparently, zero sympathy. 'You're clinging on so hard. You really never rode a horse before?'

'What gave it away?' Ryan muttered.

Reduxa brought him onwards. Morning broke with the sun on his back, and brightness warmed the hessian for a time until his smudge of vision grew deeper and the conifer smell of woodland gave way to something sweeter, and his bumpy ride finally came to a stop.

'We're here,' Licinia announced. One hand pressed against his arm and the other pulled off the bag from his head.

Ryan blinked in the light. The world around him felt unnaturally quiet. No birdsong. No drone of distant traffic, or aeroplanes flying overhead. He focused on his surroundings: an overgrown field dotted with ornate but crumbling monuments, statues and stones. Ahead stood an old, brick-built arcade perhaps ten metres long; steps at one end led into a dark tunnel entrance.

'This is a graveyard,' Ryan realised. 'Nice place for an office.'

'This cemetery was once used by the richest families and public figures of a city called Cabyllona. But when the Visigoths, the Alans and the rest settled in these parts—'

'Including the Nigels.'

'What?'

'Never mind.'

'When the barbarians settled in these parts, well, you know – there went the neighbourhood. The good Roman citizens moved away.' Licinia shrugged. 'This place hasn't been used in forty years or more.'

'Except by you.'

She looked up at him. 'The Legion has secret offices in strategic centres all over the empire. This one's my favourite, though. A fake family tomb adjoining ancient catacombs. I call it "Hidden Hall".'

'How many of you are there in this Legion of Smoke?'

'We have agents based all around the Empire.'

'And here in Gaul?'

'Me and Vitus. With basically *all* the Tenctrama gathered right here on our doorstep.' She shuddered. 'We thought at first they'd come here looking for us. But it's really the barbarians they sponsor that have brought them here. Their armies have massed just a few miles away.'

'Kind of a weird coincidence, though?'

'Yes. And I don't like coincidences.' Licinia was still looking up at him. 'Hey, I'm getting a stiff neck. Would you like a hand getting down?'

'I'm good.' Ryan took a deep breath, relaxed his arms and slid ungracefully down from Reduxa's back, landing with a stumble that almost propelled him onto his face. 'So. Is your mate here yet, with Graham?'

'I don't see his horse,' she said, tying Reduxa to a tree. 'They'll be along, I'm sure. Come with me.'

Licinia led the way into the cold, dank tunnel. Small lamps burned on the floor at intervals, enough to cast feeble light around a large, square room, supported in its centre by four pillars with long arcades on each side. Cracked stone sarcophagi stood against the far walls, crowned with carved figures in repose.

'I like what you've done with the place,' Ryan said, straight-faced. 'You don't live here, do you?'

'I live all over. I'm related to the praetorian prefect of Gaul. Vitus is a distant cousin. Our family helps govern the Gallic prefecture so we have estates all over the country.' Licinia tugged hard on the arm of one of the statues. With a hiss and an eerie creaking sound, a hidden door swung open in the brickwork.

'Don't tell me,' said Ryan, 'you've got a dog called Scoobus Doo-us in there, right?'

'You have strange ideas, Ryan.' She walked through the door, and Ryan followed her into the space beyond, which was lit with a dim green glow. 'The light comes from a substance found in the wreck of a ship of space. One built to float on the dark ether from star to star, as our own ships sail from port to port.' She looked at him, round grey eyes searching out his face, and smiled at the astonishment he couldn't hide.

'An alien spaceship?' Ryan stared. 'Back in Roman times?'

'Back in Roman times?'

'Um, figure of speech.'

'You are a man of mystery, Ryan Sinclair. If I did not have mysteries of my own I would be jealous.' Licinia pressed a particular stone in the wall and the sparkling green light grew stronger, giving a proper undersea glow to the crypt.

Ryan stared around at piles of what he could only describe as techno junk – lumps of metal with wires protruding, a crystal on a pedestal that seemed to flicker with light, a sort of stone altar which held the mummified remains of something that may or may not have been human, and stone tablets that looked like printed circuits. Dominating the far end of the hidden room was a pile of boxes stacked from dank floor to dripping ceiling, scrolls and papers spilling out from inside.

'What's all this?' Ryan asked.

Licinia struggled out of her chainmail armour; underneath she wore a simple white linen tunic, wet with sweat. 'The Legion of Smoke exists to track down, collect and collate items of supernatural and possibly extraterrestrial origin.'

'You chase after aliens and ghosts?'

'In secret.' She stared back at him, imitating his intensity. 'Interesting. The few people I've told about this either laugh in my face, or get freaked out by the idea that a small secret society know more about life's mysteries than the millions on Earth. But you? You only look … rumbled.'

'No need for an autopsy,' Ryan said quickly. 'I'm as human as you are.'

'You assume I'm human?'

'Uh …'

'Of course I am.' She laughed. 'Our patron would never have anything else on his payroll. He hates the idea of visitors from the stars, rejects the idea that supernatural events are merely natural events we don't yet understand and will do anything it takes to stop ordinary citizens – outside of the military, at least – finding out that the spooky stuff is real, it's happening. Happening all the time.'

'Take it from an ordinary citizen who found that out for himself,' said Ryan. 'Ignorance is kind of bliss. This stuff can burn. It can be dangerous. Terrible …'

'But it can also be incredible.' Licinia's eyes were the definition of that word as she looked across at him, so intense. 'When you open up to that world, let it get inside your heart … Right?'

'Right,' he whispered.

'You,' she said with a smile, 'can call me Liss.' She turned from him and started rummaging through a casket on the floor. 'Anyway, that danger, the risk of burning, is why the Legion works to confiscate any objects that could confirm the existence of creatures from other stars. We keep dangerous, terrible, amazing secrets out of the minds of mankind, locked up in depots like this around the world. Everyone, from the beggars in the street to the Senate, is left in the dark.'

'Except it's not dark when the sky's on fire, is it?' Ryan said. 'The people must know something's up.'

'The official line is that it's just a natural effect, like the northern lights. But people are still superstitious. A lot of them think it's the end of the world. And you know what?' Liss looked at him with a sad little smile. 'Sometimes I believe them.'

Chapter 12

Graham was moving more slowly now. He was exhausted from the strain of chasing around dark forests all night, and now dawn was lightening the sky his body was screaming for rest.

Something else was moaning, from nearby. It sounded like someone in pain. Graham tried to pinpoint the direction.

He crept towards a line of trees and realised it marked the edge of the wood. A thin, cracked road ran along the other side, and a thin, cracked man lay upon it, his face bruised and bloodied, snoring through a broken nose. A cloth-covered wagon lay partly in a ditch beside the road, and prints in the mud suggested the horses that pulled it had been taken; perhaps the poor sod had been mugged for his ponies? Or maybe for whatever was in his cart. It had been cleared out, now, save for some broken pots full of spice and a crust of bread. Graham gnawed at the crust hungrily, wincing at the stale, peppery taste. The bloke who'd been battered was maybe a merchant selling to soldiers wanting to sauce up their rations. He wore a deep-green cloth cloak fastened with a fancy brooch, and a tight-fitting tunic that did him no favours.

An idea occurred to Graham. In an ancient world, his muddy chinos and jacket marked him out at once as wrong and different; no wonder he and Ryan had been spotted a mile off. They needed to blend in …

Graham checked the man for broken limbs and, finding nothing conclusive, fumbled with the brooch ready to remove the cloak. The merchant's rattling breath through his bust-up nose was horrible, seeming to grow louder and more indignant as the cloak was tugged bit by bit from under him. Graham was pleased to find that the heavy material came down pretty much to his feet, hiding his shoes. As he smoothed out the cloak he felt the pot of healing gel in his jacket pocket and pulled it out.

'Where the hell are you, Doc?' Graham said sadly. 'You'd know how to get us all back together.'

The merchant broke the reverie with another bubbling breath. Graham grimaced, took the lid from the pot, dipped a finger in the cream and gently applied it to the man's swollen purple face. 'Doing us both a favour, mate. Consider it payment for the cloak. Cheers.'

'What's all this?'

Graham started, and looked up to find two Roman legionaries had appeared from the other side of the cart. They wore battered, mismatched armour, though neither had a helmet, and sported knee britches beneath their leather skirts. One had been wounded, a blood-soaked tourniquet tied round his ankle.

'Sorry to disturb you, stranger.' The able man, gaunt, bald and in his thirties, raised his sword. 'We saw the cart and hoped for medical supplies.'

'Not for me. Don't get that idea.' The injured man, black-haired and bitter, was clearly in a lot of pain and ready to inflict more. 'I mean, I can hardly walk, but what do I matter when royalty lies bleeding!'

Graham stared at the soldiers; if he could only get them on his side, they might help him find Ryan at least. 'Well … er, if it's medical supplies you're after, I'm your man. I was just helping this fella.'

'Ricimer …!' The wounded soldier was pointing at the merchant, open-mouthed.

Graham looked down and saw that the thick, purple bruising on the poor sod's face was fading so fast you could actually see it, and the broken skin was healing over.

'Magicks …' Ricimer's eyes narrowed at Graham. 'You did this?'

'Yeah. Just now.'

'What are you? A consort to those barbarian witches?'

'Nah! I told you, this is medicine, not magic. I travel around selling cures, you know?' Graham held up the little pot of ointment. 'Look, I reckon I can sort out that ankle for your mate, what's his name?'

'Zeno.'

'Well, for Zeno, I'll charge you zero. Can't say fairer, can I?'

'You speak funny,' said Zeno.

'I'm from Britannia.'

'Ahh.' Both men nodded as if this explained everything.

Ricimer looked at his friend. 'Give it a go, Zeno? Might shut you up moaning.'

'You try walking with your Achilles tendon hanging off!'

'I wouldn't let a Hun bite my foot in the first place.'

'Lads,' said Graham. 'You saw my mate's face get better. At least let me try.' *Ideally before this geezer wakes up and sees me wearing his clothes.*

Zeno limped forward and sat on the end of the cart. 'All right, Briton, you can try. But if you let me down …'

'You'll taste my sword,' said Ricimer.

'And he hasn't washed it in a while,' Zeno added.

Graham gingerly untied the blood-soaked rag around Zeno's ankle and dabbed cream across the mangled Achilles tendon.

Zeno gasped with pain. 'If you're trying to trick me—?'

'Hang on. You'll want to see this.'

Within seconds, Ricimer's eyes were out on stalks. 'I don't believe it.'

'What? It's itching like mad, but …' Zeno stared too as the wound stopped bleeding and grew less angry, scabbing over at incredible speed. 'Impossible.'

'You perform miracles.' Ricimer kicked Zeno's ankle, and smiled when Zeno put his weight on it to kick him back. 'Think of the honours Flavius Aetius will heap on us!'

'He might make us standard bearers. Double pay, Ricimer!'

'Double pay, Zeno. Let's take the Briton straight back to camp.'

'Hang on, fellas …' Graham frowned as the two legionaries closed in fast.

'I hope you've got plenty more of that balm, Briton,' Zeno hissed in his ear. 'When you're working for Rome's Commander-in-Chief, it's not wise to skimp!'

Chapter 13

Attila's encampment on the plain had incorporated the small town of Catalaunum into its defensive border; there was a checkpoint there, a unit of soldiers guarding the entrance alongside carts and tents and huge siege engines. Yaz supposed that if the Roman alliance were to break through the combined ranks of the Hunnic forces, the settlement would mark the frontier between the battlefield and the camp beyond – a flowering of colourful tents, thousands of them across the endless field. With all the loot that Attila had gathered in Gaul, the gold and silver and art treasures – not to mention the slaves, the arms, and food and fodder – the Romans must be longing to get in here.

As she and the Doctor were marched down from the ridge and into the fringes of that frontier, Yaz surveyed the defensive line. Surely, she thought, it would be suicide to attack this. Hundreds of armoured carts, laden with kegs and bags and bundles of supplies, had been wheeled into position, line after line of them arranged in a circle around the camp like a wagon-train to confound the enemy riders, to break their charge. In front of the carts had gathered hundreds of swarthy men clutching long javelins, perhaps a thousand, and a thousand more sprawled behind them; a different people, Yaz assumed, with faces painted red and yellow, carrying scythes and slingshots. Hundreds more men, in copper armour clutching long spears, were ranged behind the cart formation. She noticed enormous cages set at intervals along the defensive line, huge, wooden affairs. In the one nearest, Yaz could see grey-furred animals, wolves perhaps, apparently piled up inside on top of each other, sleeping, waiting for release.

Yes, it *would* be suicide to attack this, she thought with a chill, but thousands of young soldiers would be ordered to do so just the same, to throw away their lives on a chance of crushing the enemy. She had policed a couple of demonstrations in Sheffield, and spent the whole time imagining the chaos that would erupt if things kicked off. Here she had that same feeling only cranked up to eleven; not just because of the sheer number of those involved, but because to fight – to conquer and to kill – was the only reason they were here.

'The Battle of the Catalaunian Plains,' said the Doctor darkly as they marched on. 'Historians say it was a fight the like of which no ancient time has ever recorded. So terrible and so bloody that the ghosts of those who fell continued the struggle for three whole days and nights as violently as if they had been alive.'

'They might not have been exaggerating.' Yaz lowered her voice. 'Who won?'

'The battle wasn't decisive. Except for the estimated three hundred thousand dead.'

'In a single day?' Yaz's jaw dropped. 'Still, we're going to stop this battle, right? Avoid terrible bloodshed, save thousands of lives?'

'We can't. We mustn't.'

'Oh, what?' Yaz felt her stomach turn. 'You're not telling me it's another—'

'—fixed point in time, yes.'

'So if you stop this battle, it changes history and everything turns out differently and I was never born, and …?'

'Elvis never had a hit, butterflies step on people and cause hurricanes to flap their wings, and even really clever people mess up their analogies and, yeah. Basically, that.' The Doctor gave a forlorn shrug. 'Besides, if I did try to stop a big, old battle here on Earth, where would I stop?'

'I get it. I wish I didn't, but I do.' Yaz surveyed the colossal numbers jostling for position on the battlefield. 'So, all these people. They're going to fight today? And three hundred thousand of them will die – and then rise up again?'

'That's the bit I hope we *can* do something about.'

As they drew nearer the checkpoint, soldiers parted to allow Attila and his rescuers through. Yaz felt the men's eyes on her as they were ushered past – and then the fearful whispers as Alp marched on behind them, shunned by the rest of the party, muttering under his breath. Physically, he was bucking the typical zombie trend; there was no shambling gait, no decaying flesh, no noticeable hunger for fresh blood. His skin looked darker and shinier. Where ooze had bubbled out to block his wounds, like fat from a frying sausage, it had hardened into lumps that distorted the lines of his body, and the muscles beneath kept twitching, contracting, breaking the natural flow of his movements.

Yaz looked at the Doctor. 'Is there any chance he'll get better?'

'Better at being dead? Take it from one who knows: if you don't come back from that one at the double, you never do.'

'How can the Tenctrama be doing all this? D'you think they really are just some regular human tribe who've developed powers, or are they …?'

'Aliens?' The Doctor nodded. 'Not enough of them to make up a race – but more than enough to make up the crew of a spaceship.'

'That energy field,' Yaz realised. 'Could *that* be from a spaceship, a sort of cloaking device?'

'A sort of something,' the Doctor agreed, vaguely.

Their arrival was causing a stir of interest in more and more of the guards gathered around the opening to Catalaunum. The ripe smell of thousands of sweaty bodies and all they excreted made Yaz want to be sick – as did the jeers and catcalls from the men around them. She heard someone shout, 'Mighty Attila, you have brought us entertainment on the eve of battle?'

'Get back, dogs.' Attila tossed the snarl over his shoulder. 'Anyone who touches these two women will regret it. Clear the way.'

Another Hunnic nobleman came forward from the checkpoint; he was marked out from the rank and file by his impressive armour, leather studded with horses' hooves and antlers rising up from the shoulders. A curved sword studded with turquoise dangled at his side. There was no bowing or scraping, he simply gripped Attila's arm in firm greeting.

'At last we find you,' the man said.

'I had not thought to see you for a sentry, proud Chokona.' Attila surveyed him. 'Does the Commander of the Ten Thousand Horsemen seek a quieter life?'

'He seeks his king. Our scouts said you were coming, I wished to see for myself.'

'Attila pretended to be Commander of the Ten Thousand Horsemen!' the Doctor cried. 'Proud Chokona, that's identity theft. If you want to report him to the police, my friend Yaz will be happy to take down some particulars.'

Yaz forced an awkward smile. 'Any time.'

From beneath eyebrows as black and bushy as his ox-bow moustache, Chokona scowled at the Doctor and Yaz. 'The scouts said that Enkalo was dead, and that you bring new witches.'

'These witches have great powers,' said Attila. 'They will break this deadlock. They can do great feats that the Tenctrama cannot.'

Chokona looked unimpressed. 'Do these feats include raising an army of dead against us?'

Yaz felt her stomach clench. '*Army* of dead?'

'The Roman force tore through our blockade at the Aube,' said Chokona. 'They had beasts, like the Strava –

just as big, just as fierce. Our men fell in their hundreds and the survivors scattered, easy prey for the scum of Rome …'

The Doctor was frowning. 'Beasts like the *what* did you say?'

'Like the Strava.' Chokona pointed to the huge cage, some twenty metres away, scooped up dirt from the ground, and threw it. Dust showered through the bars – and in a heartbeat's jump a colossal creature, big as a rhino but made from wolfskin and tusks, erupted from inside and threw itself against the wooden walls. Fearful shouts and the scrape of swords against scabbards filled the air as the cage shook and teetered, and it seemed the monster might get free. Yaz backed quickly away. Only the Doctor and Alp remained: her unmoving, eyes full of concern, him twitching and whispering to himself.

'Inkri said that we alone would have the Strava.' Attila's voice was quiet and bitter. 'We held them caged in secret to maximise their impact when unleashed.'

Chokona nodded. 'Aetius has his own war-beasts and turned them loose against us. The dead were piled high. But within an hour, those that still had legs to stand on and arms to fight with were back on their feet. The Roman dead set off for their own camp, with our arrows in their backs.'

'And the dead Huns?' the Doctor demanded.

Chokona nodded back towards Catalaunum. 'The town is now their crypt.'

'Show us.' Attila strode towards the checkpoint, the Doctor, Yaz and Alp following behind. 'Now.'

Men hurried to the row of carts at the checkpoint, kicking placid oxen, driving them to shift the heavy vehicles aside. Soon Yaz was walking through the narrow streets and plain courtyards. A muttering, whispering sound drifted from the houses. Yaz looked through the dusty membrane that covered one window, and froze. The Doctor stood beside her.

Inside, she could see that the single room was crammed with soldiers, crushed upright together in a twitching mass, staring blankly and murmuring in low voices to themselves. The sight was both frightening and pathetic.

'They can use a bow,' said Chokona, 'and swing a sword, but won't kill each other.'

'Alp wouldn't even fight the dead Roman who attacked Attila.' The Doctor crossed to another house and threw open the door to reveal the rooms inside similarly rammed with the walking dead. 'My guess is that these poor remnants want to fight alongside you in real battle so they get another shot at the living enemy.'

'That will never happen.' Chokona's face was a dark twist of fury. 'These ghouls are idiot shades of the men they were. They have no place in this world.'

'No place?' the Doctor thundered. 'In this world of yours, right now, you're *all* dead men standing. You think they're idiots? Wrong. They're just bound by a certain purpose, like these Strava, I imagine: to add to the numbers fighting, to make the slaughter even worse.'

No one spoke once the Doctor had finished, until at length Attila turned to Alp. 'Go in there.' He pointed at the house whose door the Doctor had opened. 'Go on, in there! I cannot bear to see you.'

Alp turned and walked calmly into the house. He stood there as instructed, twitching and shaking like the rest. Then Chokona marched over to the door and pulled it softly closed.

'The body of a Hun warrior should be placed in the earth, facing west,' he said, 'so that he will ride to the after-life, served evermore by the souls of those he has slain in battle. Not walked into prison, brainless and babbling.'

'Placed in the earth, you said?' Yaz put a finger to her mouth. 'Listen to them. Alp and the others, they're all saying the same thing: "All together in the Great Pit".' She looked at the Doctor. 'The Pit's another word for hell, isn't it?'

'Right now, so is Catalaunum – and it's a hell of your own making.' The Doctor glared at Attila, the whispering of the dead like a hopeless lullaby beneath her words. 'You agreed to dance with the devil. Are you really so surprised to find she's been calling the tune all along?'

Attila locked eyes with her. 'I will hold Inkri to account.'

'And I wouldn't miss her explanations for all the world.' The ghost of a smile played around the Doctor's face. 'Shall we?'

Chapter 14

Ryan was getting bored in the Hidden Hall, while Liss searched through her files for something she claimed would rock his world. All he could think about were his friends, somewhere out there in this land of secret histories.

'How long have the Tenctrama been around?' he asked. 'When did you find out about them?'

'Rumours that there were real witches helping the barbarians began forty years ago, when Rome was sacked by the Visigoths. But they go back further. Way further.'

'When did you find out? How'd you get a job with the Legion of Smoke anyway?'

'You inherit it. Barring accidents, the eldest born becomes the next member of the Legion.'

'You can't say no?'

'You caught what I said about "barring accidents", right?' Liss picked up and studied an egg-shaped device. 'When my father died, I was initiated, I learned about his real work. That was six years ago.' She fitted a metal sheath over the egg. 'Vitus was already here, he helped train me.

By then the existence of the Tenctrama and their powers was well known. The stories had spread.'

'Bet your boss didn't like that.'

'At first, we were supposed to prove that the witches were fakes. Trouble is, they're *not* fakes.' Liss plonked both egg and sheath into a stone casket and shook her head. 'War's always been horrific, everyone knows that, but with the Tenctrama casting their combat magicks …'

'It's worse.' Ryan nodded with feeling. 'So what can we do about it? I mean, the Legion wants my help, right?'

'It did when it thought you had some decent tech.' Liss's smile was small, but it was a start. 'All we can do is keep looking for a way to match or overcome their powers. We have a small number of weapons from the stars—'

'What, and you haven't used them?'

'We're not sure how to,' she confessed. 'And even if we could get close enough to try, what reprisals would we risk?'

Ryan supposed that made sense. 'And if you're keeping all this tech-stuff secret, you might draw a bit of attention.'

Liss nodded. 'Even our master knows nothing of the weapons. If he were to use them – in war, or in peace – we might have worse problems than the Tenctrama.'

'Absolute power corrupts absolutely?'

'Ooh, that's good. You are wise, Ryan.' Her face had fallen again. 'Vitus and I have been searching every depot for some small weakness in these witches, poring over every arcane book the Legion has collected, every cylinder of stamped clay, every scrap of occult ritual hunted out from the edges of our empire and beyond, from the seers of Babylon to the desert-priests beyond Volubilis.'

'Have you found anything?'

'No!' she shouted, the word echoing hard off the glowing walls.

'Wrong,' Ryan said, with the smallest smile. 'You found me, and Graham. And we've got friends out there you're going to want to meet, cos they can help. Properly. Honest.' He paused. 'See, the Doctor is, like, an expert in stuff like this. She travels in the sort of ship where you found these creepy light effects. It looks like a blue box from the outside, but it's her TARDIS and she—'

'*What* did you say?' Liss jumped up. 'Doctor? TARDIS? You're messing with me.'

'What—?'

She stared at him. 'Say you're messing with me and I'll mess with your beautiful face, Ryan Sinclair.'

'God, calm down, I'm not messing!' Ryan protested. 'What do you know about the TARDIS, then – and the Doctor?'

'What do I know!' Liss rubbed her hands together, eyes bright. 'Hundreds of years ago, when Nero was Emperor, a blue casket marked with strange writing was found at the bottom of a cliff some distance from Rome. It looked to be a sarcophagus made of wood but could not be marked in any way by any tool, nor forced open. The Legion made arrangements to confiscate it, but by the time this had been arranged, the blue box had disappeared. Not taken – *disappeared*. There were no marks in the ground save for four sets of strange footprints, leading to the place where this box had lain for weeks, at least.' She was clearly relishing the mystery of her tale. 'A member of the Legion saw it again some fifteen years later, investigating supernatural events in Pompeii, just before Mount Vesuvius erupted. Then, a further thirty years later, the likeness of the blue casket was seen yet again – this time as a statue in a house in Rome, a temple named as TARDIS. The effigies of household gods, a man and a woman, stood beside it. I've seen the rubbings, they're kept in the depot at Ravenna.'

'Well mysterious,' said Ryan, wondering what lucky fella had been travelling with the Doctor in those days. 'Well, you're right about the blue casket. It disappears from one place, and reappears in another.'

'A ghostly casket?' Liss's smile was childlike. 'But it is so small, what mechanism could possibly fit inside to make it move?'

'It's bigger on the inside. Like Pandora's box, or jar, or whatever you said, only full of good stuff—'

'I told you, and I wasn't lying, I will mess with your face.' She took his cheeks in her hands and smooshed them. 'You've been *inside* the blue casket?'

'Yeah.' As well as weirded out, Ryan felt truly proud. He pulled her hands away, and held on to them. 'My friends and me, we've been all over in it. And we really can help. That's why you've got to help me find her, and Yaz, and Graham—'

'Oh, we'll help you,' Liss said. 'Vitus will be back soon, I know, and then …' Standing on tiptoes she kissed Ryan wetly on the side of his mouth. 'Oh, I feel giddy!'

Ryan felt quite giddy himself but tried to play things cool. 'Yeah?'

'It's hope, that's what it is. Hope.'

'Hope that you get to kiss me again?'

'Of course I do.' She kissed him at once on the other side of his mouth. 'This thing with the Tenctrama … it's been going on for so long. For ages, actual ages. And you see, I was the one who made the discovery.'

The thought of the hovering hags put chills up Ryan's spine, wrecking the moment. 'What discovery?'

'It's stopped me sleeping pretty much ever since.' Liss rushed over to an ornate casket placed against the wall, lifted its lid and sorted clumsily through the contents. 'You know, it was all so much easier in the old days when people believed in many gods. You could blame so much strangeness on them. Now we just have the one, all-powerful lord who claims a monopoly on miracles. Perhaps that is why the Tenctrama moved on from targeting Rome to seduce the pagan barbarians with their powers.'

'They targeted Rome first?' He watched her sorting through the endless scrolls. 'What are you looking for? Can I help you find it?'

'Got it.' She held up some crumbling parchments and studied them. 'The story goes back to the Sibylline books.'

'Sibyl who?'

'*Sibylline*,' she corrected him. 'God, you're so backward in Britannia. The Sybils were prophetesses, keepers of temples, bridges between the world of the living and the land of the dead. They'd write prophecies on oak leaves.

You know, *vague* prophecies. You could read pretty much anything into them, you know? But one of these Sibyls was different.'

'Yeah?' Ryan sensed another story coming on. 'Different how?'

'The legends say that, about a thousand years ago, a Sybil came to the court of the last royal of the Roman Kingdom, Tarquin the Proud, with nine books said to embody all the secrets of human destiny. Predictions of just what was coming down the centuries for Rome. She said she'd sell him the nine books but the price was enormous and Tarquin said no. So, the Sybil threw three of the books on the fire. She demanded exactly the same price for the remaining six. Old Tarquin was sweating now, but he refused again …'

Ryan guessed where this was going. 'So she threw another one on the fire?'

'Another *three*. Only three books left now. And *still* she wanted the same price.' Liss tutted. 'Tarquin caved. Paid up in full. Although, I don't think it was the money she wanted. It was his belief.'

'Well, were the books any good?'

'Not for Tarquin the Proud,' said Liss wryly. 'They foretold that his reign would quickly come to an end, and it did. The Senate took charge, and the books were kept in a stone chest underground in the Temple of Jupiter on Capitoline Hill. Fifteen patricians from the ruling families, handpicked by a secret inner council of the Senate, were made the books' guardians. Only they were allowed to consult the books and learn their secrets; that was the origin of the Legion of Smoke.' Now she produced a purple, cylindrical wooden box. 'This is one of the original books.'

Ryan felt a tickle down his spine as he eyed the several blackened rolls of parchment inside.

Licinia reached in and took one. Holding it in her right hand she unrolled it with her left. 'As is custom, there is a portrait of the book's author on the first page. Perhaps you might recognise this prophetess of human destinies …?'

Ryan saw, with a chill, the face he'd never wanted to see again. The twisted, unnatural features of the witch-woman from the forest. It was her, no question, staring back at him from a thousand years ago, a knowing smile scoring one more wrinkle in that hideous face.

Chapter 15

Marched through the Roman army camp by Zeno and Ricimer, Graham felt as though he were pushing through the pages of a school history textbook. He'd coloured pictures of Roman army tents as a kid, using bright orange pencils. Now to be walking among the endless lines of leather tents, each three metres square and lined up with suitably military precision, so close together that the guy ropes overlapped ... It was surreal and scary and brilliant all in one.

The sheer scale of the camp! From swathes of Roman uniformity to the colour clashes of the brighter barbarian tents across the field, it seemed impossible that such a place could pop up overnight. The stink of it – manure, smoke, urine, unwashed bodies – was everywhere, overpowering.

Senses overloaded, it was small details that caught in his mind later – servants asleep on a pile of armour outside the tent. Bloodied survivors of last night's skirmish sat in huddles, ignored by all. The staggering whiff and hubbub of the toilet block, fenced in by felled trees, the hastily gouged channel in the mud through to a stagnant stream piled high with ...

Yeah, I'll hold it in, thanks, Graham thought.

The strangest sight was soldiers gathering wheat in a cordoned area that seemed freshly dug over. He looked between Zeno and Ricimer. 'Bit of luck, isn't it – finding crops already growing here?'

'They weren't,' said Zeno, who'd lost pretty much all of his limp by now. 'The Tenctrama have a grain that grows quickly.'

'What, *that* quickly?' Graham stared at the stalks in the ground. He could almost see new growth.

'We add water and the crushed grains make gruel.' Ricimer patted his stomach. 'It tastes like sick. But soldiers can't fight on empty bellies.'

'Guess they can't.' Graham shook his head, surprised his healing gel had drawn any attention at all among the miracles of these witch-women.

Zeno and Ricimer brought him straight to the First Centurion's tent – spacious but still smelly – and told their story. The centurion was in a right old mood, he'd been trying to grab some sleep. 'This had better be on the level,' he warned the legionaries, 'or you'll be mucking out the Strava.' Whatever that meant, the two legionaries didn't look happy as, together, they waited for word of Graham's marvellous medicine to be taken to Flavius Aetius himself.

Within minutes, Graham had been granted audience. But Zeno and Ricimer were in for a let-down. 'You two,' the First Centurion said, 'report to the obstacle trenches and relieve the guards on the dead.'

'Tell the old man how quickly we brought you here, Briton,' Ricimer hissed.

Zeno nodded. 'We deserve a reward.'

'You deserve the blockhouse,' the First Centurion shouted. 'And keep quiet about all this, or you'll be digging latrines instead!'

Graham gave a sombre salute to his escorts then found himself taken at speed to a much larger tent, this one built around poles with a peaked roof perhaps three metres high, the mules that must carry it tethered just outside. Along the way he tried to gather his thoughts, aware that the safety of his friends – and his own – was riding on this meeting. A meeting with Aetius! The final great leader of the Roman empire in the west. *Treat him like a regular bloke,* Graham told himself. *He still wipes his bum like the rest of us. Well, maybe with a sponge on a stick instead of paper, but …*

'Consus,' the Centurion called at the tent flap, 'your master sent for this … visitor.'

A small, slight man with doleful features too big for his face appeared in the entrance. Consus gestured that Graham should join him inside. Aetius's tent was impressive inside as well as out, with chairs, a desk half-buried under scrolls and their containers, tapestries hanging from the walls and almost tropical heat from a huge vat filled with hot water half hidden by canvas screens.

Great, thought Graham, *I've interrupted bath-time.*

A squat, muscular man in his late fifties walked out casually from behind the screens, stark naked. Graham reddened and looked away at once, keeping his gaze on Consus as the slave applied a perfumed lotion to his master's back. His first thought was *Whoa …!* On reflection, he realised that this was most likely intimidation tactics:

suggesting that Graham mattered so little to this noble of Rome, he wasn't even worth dressing for.

'I am the Patrician Flavius Aetius, Master of Soldiers.' The man's voice was deep and measured, and he studied a dagger in its hilt placed on his dresser while Consus selected a tunic for him to wear. 'You're the medic from Britain?'

'Graham O'Brien, sir.'

Consus made Aetius decent with a linen loincloth, thank God, and laid out a tough-looking leather skirt that was burnished with gold. Aetius considered the kilt, then looked up at Graham – his eyes were a pure, pale blue, cold as stones beneath a short fringe of greying hair. 'You have a medicine that can cure wounds swiftly, I understand?'

'That's right.'

'Prove it.' Aetius took the dagger and casually sliced into his slave's upper arm. Consus cried out and then stared in shock at the blood trickling down his arm, while his master gripped him firmly by the back of the neck to stop him moving. Graham swore under his breath and kept swearing as he grabbed the pot of gel, wiped some of the blood from the cut with his cloak and then quickly applied the medication while the poor slave writhed in pain. Aetius watched Graham coldly as he worked.

Get on with it! Graham willed the gel to close the cut before this poor bloke bled out. *Come on, crazy cream, do your thing.*

After what felt like an age, Consus's cut began to scab stickily over. Graham puffed out a massive sigh of relief. 'There you go, son.'

'Congratulations.' Aetius released his slave, who fell panting to his knees.

'Was that really necessary?' Graham asked.

'Bathing between battles is a luxury I indulge, and I had no wish to dirty more clothes with the blood of my dresser.'

That's not what I meant, Graham wanted to say, but Aetius was already turning to his slave as if nothing had happened: 'I'll have the red and gold beneath the breastplate today.' Consus, pale and sweaty, got up, bowed and hurried to obey, poor sod.

'This medication works uncannily fast,' Aetius observed. 'It's not magick?'

'Oh no, guv. No way. Science.'

'And what is in this remarkable medicine?'

'Well …' Graham racked his brain. 'It's the eleven secret herbs and spices. Fifty-seven varieties of, er, beans—'

'No matter. Time is brief.' The pause that followed was brief too. 'I require your services with another patient whose condition is … serious. You will be rewarded if you accept. Flogged if you do not.'

'Well, that's a kind offer.' Graham pulled himself up to his full height, tugged at his cloak. 'But what I really need is some help from you.'

'Oh, really?' Aetius's rich voice dropped to a dangerous whisper. 'How may I be of service?'

'I lost three friends in the woods a few miles from here. I need help finding them.'

Aetius's upper lip curled. 'You may not have noticed, but I'm soon to commit to the bloodiest battle of my long career. My forces are taking up positions on the field even now, ready to clash with three hundred thousand Huns, and you want me to break off to find three Britons loose in the countryside?'

'Yeah! Cos they've got to be in danger. I've seen the dead rise up and fight out there in those woods, and the Huns are out there—'

'There are no marauding dead!' Aetius snapped. 'That's fake news.'

'Oh, yeah? What about the Legion of Smoke, then? Vitus and his mate are fakes too, are they?'

Aetius's eyes widened. 'You can't know of these things!'

'I know about the Tenctrama too, helping out your barbarian armies,' Graham retorted, all the pent-up emotion rushing out in anger. 'You gonna pretend they've got nothing to do with all this, are you?'

Across the tent, Consus was staring at Graham as if he had two heads, and was about to lose them both. Graham bit his tongue: *You idiot, you've gone too far.* He could hear Grace in his ear: *You get so tetchy when you're scared …*

'I would like to hear you explain,' said Aetius slowly, 'how a medic from Britannia knows of such uncommonly dangerous things.'

Graham managed a smile of apology. 'Mostly from trying to avoid them.'

'Would that we could. But time presses and you must help me resolve a delicate situation. The future of Rome and all the civilised world may hang in the balance.' The General's blue eyes were untouched by the twitch of a smile on his face. 'No pressure.'

Chapter 16

'A thousand years ...' Ryan closed up the Sibylline book so he didn't have to look at that hideous Tenctrama face. 'How can it be the same person all that time later?'

'Perhaps it's just a close resemblance,' said Liss. 'Perhaps the Tenctrama hibernate. Or they can shapeshift?'

'Or they've got a whole lot of staying power,' Ryan suggested. 'How come you've got one of these books, anyway?'

'The Legion has all of them.' Liss shrugged. 'They were confiscated when Rome turned to Christianity and the temples were closed, but by then the predictions had run out and the Tenctrama had long since left Rome.'

'To go where?'

'Their likeness appears on pottery and in tapestries found in Africa, Britannia, the Steppes of the east ...' Liss tapped the scroll. 'Perhaps they made prophecies there too.'

'They really saw into the future?'

'They gave no warnings of natural disasters, like the great wave that destroyed the port at Ostia, or Vesuvius erupting. But they did predict the Antonine plague that killed up to two thousand each day at its worst … and they seem to foretell the sack of Rome by the Senone Gauls, the wars against the Samnites, the Macedonian Wars …'

'Big on battles,' said Ryan. 'Big on death.'

'Some of their predictions were years out. But many were accurate.' Again, Liss opened the scroll and scanned it. 'They foretold that special seeds would be discovered in the valley of the River Liri in the wake of the first Samnite war … crops that would grow even on stony ground, and feed the masses for ever. If the seeds were sown in specific locations across the empire and beyond, the empire of Rome would never fall. So of course, the Emperor sent out scouts and, sure enough, the seeds were found and they were planted out as foretold, and they have flowered ever since.'

'So, the Tenctrama weren't only predicting the future,' said Ryan, 'they could've been, like, *guiding* the future. Making it happen. I mean, if the Tenctrama live for ages, they might have said that a war was coming, then started it themselves – and then dumped the seeds afterwards ready to be discovered?'

Liss nodded slowly. 'That's what I think. We can see they're manipulating military empires even now. They're just not bothering to do it in secret.'

'Wonder what's changed? Are the crops from those seeds still feeding people?'

'Yes. They have been for centuries.'

'So basically the Tenctrama have got you eating their crops as well as fighting their battles.' Ryan looked at her. 'But what's it all for?'

Suddenly there was a scraping noise from the wall.

'Quickly.' Liss pulled Ryan into a small alcove beside the shelves filled with scrolls, pressed up against him in the narrow space. But there was nothing fun or flirtatious in her face now.

They heard the door grind slowly open.

Yaz had that horrible sense of impending doom as she was herded through the camp beside the Doctor. Men cheered at the sight of their king back walking among them, and Attila beamed radiantly, raising his arms, a magnetic, powerful presence. As he passed, men and women worked with renewed effort, eager to show their commitment. The whole of the camp seemed bent on the work of war, their faces as fierce as the longing to stay alive. Everywhere she looked, people were polishing weapons, sharpening swords, braiding bowstrings, reinforcing battle jackets with metal scales, or lining helmets, or putting new leather on saddles. Horses stood about in full trappings, stable boys attending them like pit-stop mechanics around performance motors. The ring of the smiths' hammers on anvils sounded ominously through the camp like a bell of doom.

'Prepare yourselves, witches.' Attila tossed a casual glance back at them. 'Inkri has been summoned to my tent.'

Yaz's expectations of the word 'tent' left her unprepared for the sight that awaited her. Rearing up ahead of her stood a palace plucked from some delirious romance, fully four storeys high. The walls were formed from cream-and-red-striped felt hung over thick wooden flats, the structure held strong by towering golden pillars grooved into place. A large flag, with a sun picked out in gold and a sword in scarlet, billowed over wooden ramparts. The double doors were decorated with white horsetails and golden spheres, each as big as Yaz's fists, and guarded by two frightening, barrel-chested men whose heads bore more scars than features. On the black bearskin hats shone a silver star.

'When he said "tent", I was imagining my two-person job on a rainy night out in the Peak District,' said Yaz. 'Bit more upmarket.'

'This is definitely glamping,' the Doctor agreed.

The guards at the door lowered their heads, and the bigger of the two reported, 'Inkri waits within.'

Yaz looked at the Doctor, full of nerves. 'Here goes, then. We're going to meet a Tenctrama.'

The Doctor placed a hand on her shoulder and smiled. 'Isn't she lucky?'

The guards stepped away from the door, their looks as sharp as their daggers, as Attila strode into the huge tent and into cool shade. The air was filled with spice and incense, but a sickly reek of decay still lingered.

The tent stretched back perhaps thirty feet, and a long table surrounded by ornately carved chairs dominated the space. The floor was a thick rug made of coconut fibres. The windows had no glass but transparent membranes, some poor animal's innards, she supposed; the cloudy sky outside made them look like blocks of ice. Magnificent swords hung from the thick felt covering the walls, the largest of which had been placed behind the largest chair with the tallest back, clearly Attila's throne. Yaz blinked, and saw suddenly that something perched upon it: a hunched creature with matted grey hair that hung down in clumps over a pinched and sallow face.

Inkri.

Chapter 17

Yaz's skin crawled just at the sight of the Tenctrama witch-woman. The rotting smell grew stronger, and the fear she felt was deep and instinctive.

The woman on the throne turned her lopsided face towards Attila. Her eyes were clouded but still glittered gold. Eyelashes stretched down from the jutting lower lids like long scratches in the wrinkled face. The toothless smile was like a crack in sun-dried earth.

Attila stared at the figure with undisguised disgust. 'Get up from my throne, witch. We are due a reckoning.'

'Oh, my proud warrior.' Inkri went on smiling as she talked, her long fingers flexing and twitching. 'My deeds, my powers, my counsel – they have brought you this throne, great king, and the glory you have enjoyed. Our account is long since settled.'

'Ah, yes, now, about that …' The Doctor strode forward, grinning like this was afternoon tea in a country house, and held out her hand to shake. 'Sorry, not been introduced, I'm the Doctor, Mr Hun's new attorney. I'd like to go over the terms of this settlement …'

Inkri ignored her entirely, but Attila didn't. 'Doctor, this is a matter for me alone,' he warned, 'you will be silent.'

'I will? Nah, can't see that happening.' She turned back to the Tenctrama. 'There again, perhaps I'm not as good at predicting the future – or engineering it – as our fascinating friend here. Where are you from, then, Inkri? Because you're not from Earth, are you?'

'She is from the dead lands,' said Attila, advancing. 'She has stolen the souls of great warriors and bewitched their bodies.'

'More accurately, she has the ability to manipulate and reanimate necrotic tissue.'

Yaz saw Attila's face darken in confusion. 'The Tenctrama are good with dead stuff,' she said quickly.

'The dead are another Tenctrama gift for you, my king,' said Inkri, as if the Doctor and Yaz weren't even there. 'Their sinew will bring strength to your sword, the better to slay your enemies.'

'My enemies, yes – and your sisters give the same boon to them!'

'They do.' Inkri looked at Attila steadily. 'But I have matched their powers, all these years, kept the Huns on a level footing.' She paused, took a wheezing breath. 'Imagine had I not.'

'Insolent hag.' Attila charged forward, gripped the withered creature by the arm and hauled her bodily from the throne, shouting in her face. 'I have other witches now.' He nodded to the Doctor and Yaz. 'They possess magicks that do not make monsters of fallen men.' He threw the wizened creature to the floor in front of the throne. 'No Hun ever flinched from wounds in battle. At birth, our cheeks are pierced with swords – we taste pain and blood before we know our mother's milk. But how can any soldiers fight well knowing what their deaths will make of them?'

'You lack faith, Attila,' Inkri hissed, rising up slowly with a sound like dead leaves rustling. 'Long ago, I told you, and your father before you – in this struggle, only when the dead outnumber the living can final triumph come.'

'But triumph for who?' The Doctor was still staring at the Tenctrama, fascinated. 'There're two sides to everything, aren't there, Inkri? You and your people have been "helping" the rulers of these empires achieve their goals, by making them better at war. Widening the scope of battle, escalating the weaponry, increasing the casualties.' She moved closer. 'But here are the things I wanna know: where are you from? What are you doing here?'

'How many of you are there?' Yaz said, finding her voice.

'Good question, Yaz! Sorry, this is Yasmin Khan, she's my bestie. You have besties in the Tenctrama?'

Yaz saw the withered form vanish, like there was a jump cut in reality. Suddenly, that hideous lopsided face was right up in front of her own, eyes blazing, breath like a draught from an abattoir. 'Yasmin Khan …' Inkri's thin, yellow lips quivered as if tasting the words, her smile growing larger. 'It shall be a pleasure to learn more of you, child.'

The empty mouth widened to laugh or scream or swallow her.

With a shout, Yaz fell back against the table, shaking. The Doctor rushed to her, eyes big like a puppy's. 'What happened? You all right?'

'I … don't know.' When Yaz looked, Inkri was not such a pathetic figure as before. She was standing in front of the throne, gazing straight at her, the smile still a split in her face. 'It was weird, I thought she moved. I'm not even sure what she said.'

'Care to repeat?' The Doctor looked coldly at Inkri as she helped Yaz up and into one of the chairs at the big table. 'How about you, Attila, d'you hear … anything at all?' She crossed to where the Hun now stood immobile, his dark eyes blank. She waved her hand in front of him but he did not react. 'What is that, a light hypnotic trance?'

Then the image froze in Yaz's head.

The Doctor caught her friend's blank expression. 'Oh, no! You too, Yaz?'

Inkri's voice was brittle. 'Now we can speak freely, Doctor.'

The Doctor turned to face Inkri, and found the Tenctrama had moved silently, was standing just behind her. She didn't flinch. 'Let Yasmin go.'

'In time,' said Inkri.

'Am I supposed to be impressed by your powers? Should I gasp, or swoon?' The Doctor affected a fainting spell, fell into a chair, swung up her legs and plonked them on Attila's council table. 'It stands to reason: if you Tenctrama can switch on the brains of the human dead, why shouldn't you be able to switch off the brains of the living? Low-level telepathic field, is it? Enough to control and direct a flock of birds – or plant a thought or two in somebody's head.'

'You are plainly not of this world,' Inkri said softly. 'Why do you care for these animals?'

'P'raps because, out of all the life forms I've ever met, human beings are the … lifiest.' The Doctor swung her legs off the table and leaned forward. 'Here's how it is. I don't only care about the people of this planet. I happen to protect them.'

'Yet they war among themselves so freely.'

'They also love so freely. And they fight for what they believe is right even when they're pitifully wrong. I can't save them from themselves, Inkri, but I can protect them from the likes of you – creatures infiltrating their power hierarchies by stealth and doing their best to slaughter them all.' The Doctor got up, pushed her hands into her pockets, and bent down until she was Inkri's height. 'Seems you've been playing a long game here, and I'm sorry to barge in before it's finished to call you in for bedtime, but actually, not sorry. And guess what, I'm giving you the chance to do what these humans can't and stop yourselves – before *I* stop you.'

'Threats from a child?' Inkri held the Doctor's gaze. 'You have no idea who we are.'

'And you don't have much of an idea who *I* am, for all your efforts to probe my unconscious mind back in the forest. Or you'd know my childhood was a very long time ago.'

'You measure lifespan in a few thousand years,' Inkri looked amused, 'and think you are *not* a child?'

'We just don't seem to know what each other's about, do we?' The Doctor grinned suddenly. 'Hey! How about we take turns guessing? OK, I'll start. I think … that the Tenctrama feed on the psychic energy generated by fear and hate and anger, that's why you're stirring up the fighting. Am I warm?'

'Cold,' said Yaz. 'So cold.' The word sounded drawn from her lips like a yawn.

The Doctor shook her head. 'Don't do that.'

'No?' Inkri lowered her voice to a menacing whisper. 'I think you care very much for the three friends you brought with you.'

'Is that your guess? Well done. Not just warm, but boiling hot. Like the water you'll find yourself in if you mess with any of my friends again.'

'You think we fear war with you, Doctor?'

'Hey, not fair, that's another guess and you already had a turn.'

'I will show you how little I fear death.' Inkri looked at Attila and, as if a spell had been broken, he started forward, confused for a moment. Yaz was still silent and staring though – and Inkri was back on the chair as if she'd never moved.

'Did you enjoy your rest, my king?' came the sepulchral voice.

'You made me sleep,' Attila growled, slapping his temples with the flats of both hands. 'Witch, I forbade you to work your magicks on me.'

'But I know you so well after all these years. It is so easy to steal inside your silly little mind.' She chuckled, a sound dry and mirthless. 'How can you be certain which are your own thoughts and which I have given you?'

The Doctor felt uneasy. *Why is she provoking him?*

'I warn you, witch,' Attila's voice filled the room like the buzz of a wasp, his beady eyes fixed on her. 'The Doctor has magicks that you and your brethren cannot match. With those powers I can destroy you, Aetius and all his rabble. And no one will be bringing you back from the dead.'

'Oh, but they will.' In a blink and a blur, Inkri was suddenly upon him, her face twisted by her leering smile, muscles quivering beneath the leathered flesh. Her voice deepened further to a supernatural bellow: *'YOU WILL BRING US BACK.'*

Instinct bit Attila, and he drew his sword.

'Don't!' the Doctor shouted, starting forward.

But the blade had already swung up, slicing through the Tenctrama's scrawny neck. The Doctor recoiled as a blinding light spilled and stretched from the wizened wound like glowing strands of cobweb, blasting out through the tent in a kind of luminous grid over the battlespace beyond.

'I ... I killed her,' Attila said.

'You did something.' The Doctor ran to the doorway in time to see the light trails fading like fireworks, the guards at the door staring up in mute disbelief.

'Oh, my ...' Yaz staggered over to the Doctor's side. 'What happened to me? I could hear voices, but I couldn't see, it was like I was trapped in my own head. Like something ... hungry was outside.'

The Doctor squeezed her shoulder. 'It's over. For now, anyway.'

As she spoke, that same unearthly golden brightness shone high overhead, just as it had done the night before.

'Uh-oh,' Yaz said, shielding her eyes from the brilliant buzz of the clouds.

'The return of that atmospheric excitation.' The Doctor looked troubled in the ashen radiance. 'A parting shot?'

'I can understand this glow coming on at night, when it's dark, to help them see to fight. But why would the Tenctrama start it up in broad daylight?'

'Light doesn't just help things to see, does it?' The Doctor's eyes held Yaz's. 'It helps things to grow.'

'Enough, Doctor.' Attila turned to face her, his eyes black as flies. 'I have need of you, or else you would be dead for the disrespect you have shown me. Yasmin shall remain under guard to ensure you do as I ask.'

The Doctor rolled her eyes. 'And what you ask is for me to win you this battle with my mighty magicks?'

'I require your rod of crystal that laid waste to the forest.'

'It's out of charge, kaput! You know that.'

'You may use your magick wand to repair it. However! Should you use it against any Hun, or try to escape, or do anything that displeases me – I will kill Yasmin Khan, witch or not.' He smiled. 'And now the Tenctrama have gone, at least she will stay dead.'

'You sound very sure of that.' The Doctor went on staring up at the glowing sky, remembering Inkri's words. 'Only, how do you know that's your own thought, and not one the Tenctrama have given you?'

Chapter 18

Graham looked down gingerly at his patient lying on the patterned mat: a wiry man in his forties with flowing grey hair. His face was round and his nose thin and curved, brows bunched over his shut-tight eyes against the pain of his wounds. There was a nasty-looking gash in his belly; the man coughed violently, groaning and thrashing from side to side. Looking away, Graham noticed the man's left knee was mangled and swollen.

Ridiculously, the theme tune from *Quincy, ME* started playing in Graham's head. 'Come on,' he muttered. 'He's not dead yet.'

'A brilliant diagnosis,' Aetius said dryly. 'Now, hurry, man, his attendants will not tolerate leaving him for long. This isn't some Gallic peasant, it's the Visigoth king, Theodoric – and I can't afford for him to die!'

Right royal bedside manner, thought Graham. 'I'll need to scrub up a bit.' He looked at his dirty hands, very much at odds with the fine fur robe that Aetius had draped over his appropriated cloak; this patient was too important to be attended by a mere commoner and so Graham had become an honorary nobleman, escorted to this spacious tent by the mighty Roman himself. Brightly coloured sashes had been pinned to the leather walls and plant garlands placed on the floor along with healing prayers scrawled on slates. Graham reached towards a stone basin beside the patient but found it dark with something floating in it. 'What's this?'

'His wound has been treated with unwashed wool dipped in wine and vinegar.'

'What quack thought *that* was a good idea?'

'My personal physician,' Aetius said coldly, 'working from the collected wisdoms of Pliny the Elder.'

'Oh. Right.' Graham sighed and pulled out the little pot of gel. 'Well, anyway. How'd King Theodoric end up like this?'

'He took a Hun javelin to his gut as we broke the barricade on the Aube.' Aetius paced impatiently. 'The Visigoths' Tenctrama witch said there was nothing she could do for him, that his people should be glad because soon he would rise again and endure for ever. But Theodoric isn't so keen on becoming a "mumbling vegetable with demons under his skin", so I suggested that if magicks could not save him, perhaps reason and science might.'

'And unwashed wool, gotcha. Explains why your boys were out for medical supplies when they found me.' Graham started smearing the gel over the stomach wound as deftly as he could. 'Only, I don't get it. The Visigoths are barbarians, aren't they? Like the Huns. How come they're fighting on your side, and not Attila's?'

'We may hate each other, but we hate Attila more. He wants the world under his boot and, if no one stands against him, Attila's forces will sweep on into Gaul and beyond unchecked.' Aetius looked as though he carried the weight of the empire on his shoulders, and Graham supposed that the poor sod did. 'Should Attila and his witches topple the Emperor and make his capital in Rome, then superstition and chaos shall eclipse the sweet order of Roman rule. Centuries of civilisation and culture shall be destroyed and nothing but blood, fire and dust take its place.'

'And you couldn't stop him without some hairy help?'

'The army of Rome is weak and ill-disciplined. We could not defend our territory from the Visigoths and the other Germanic tribes and so we granted them space to settle and made trade agreements. When Attila marched into Gaul, they faced a choice – to fight alongside Rome or see their adopted land devastated by the Huns. They chose Rome. But I know these people, I have lived among them, fought in their armies; the barbarian who stands with me today could turn on me tomorrow.'

'And in any case, their help comes with Tenctrama strings attached, right? Now I get why you want to cure this bloke so badly.' Graham cleaned out the bottom of the pot with his fingertip and applied it to the royal knee. 'If *you* save the Visigoth king, he owes you a big one, right?'

'You grasp my stratagem.' Aetius gave a tight smile. 'I will have achieved what the Tenctrama could not.'

'So you reckon he'll ditch the witches and keep in with you.'

'That is my hope. The barbarians are strong enough already but with the Tenctrama in their ranks?' He scowled. 'They have turned the necessity of battle into something depraved. The fighting grows madder and bloodier with no victors ...'

Theodoric writhed and groaned and, as his stomach muscles tightened, Graham saw that the flesh around the wound was knitting back together. He puffed out his cheeks with relief. 'Reckon the king's won his own little battle, anyway.'

A voice broke in from just outside the tent. 'That's enough, lad.' It was the First Centurion, who'd been given orders to stand guard and allow no one entry. 'You're paid as a soldier, try to act like one.'

'You weren't there, sir. You didn't see it!'

Theodoric groaned, more softly but still in distress. Aetius rose crossly and yanked open the tent flap. 'Centurion, what is the meaning of this disturbance?'

A young legionary, panting for breath and frightened out of his wits, stood in the centurion's grip. 'Sir, I had to warn you. Attila has found another witch. A stronger witch than the Tenctrama. I've seen her!'

Aetius signalled that the Centurion should release the newcomer. 'Explain yourself.'

'Attila lives, sir. Our scouts sighted him, we tried to ambush his party on the approach to the Hun camp. But his new witch has a wand that sets swords and armour ablaze. With a single touch she threw me through the air!'

Graham's heart did its own re-enactment. "Ere, did she have blonde hair and was she wearing a rainbow?

Was there anyone with her – a pretty girl, maybe, a black lad …?'

'There was a dark-skinned fighting girl with her.'

'That's the Doctor and Yaz! They're all right!' Graham's grin faltered. 'Wait, they're with Attila?'

'And a dead Hun who killed three of us. Three of us who followed me back to camp.' The legionary kept nodding like his neck was rubber. 'This new witch, sir. It must be she who flattened the forest.'

Aetius stared. 'She did what?'

'Levelled the entire northwest corner. Even the grass was torn away.'

'The lads on the last Search and Destroy trip corroborate this story, sir,' said the First Centurion, looking troubled. 'They say the whole of Gaul shook and trees were shrugged from the ground like fleas from a dog's back.'

'So.' Aetius rounded on Graham. 'These are the innocent friends you would have me find?'

Graham cringed from the anger in those cold blue eyes. 'Well, two of them, Chief, yeah.'

'And what scientific explanations do you propose for your Doctor's deeds, eh, Briton?' He shook his head and started to pace. 'I was a fool to think your medicine came from science. I imagine that, even now, your friend is granting Attila supernatural powers for the coming battle.'

'She wouldn't help the Huns! She's their prisoner.'

'You are mine, and you have done as I told you.'

'To try and save a man's life!'

'Yes. Your own.' Aetius looked over to the hazy movement of the Hun camp across the plain. 'What does your friend plan for us, hmm? What is she capable of?'

The First Centurion looked out of his depth. 'Do you still want to commit to taking the hill on the plains ahead of the Huns, sir? Our scouts report they're arranging their forces.'

'Have the watch kept and wait for my command,' said Aetius. 'I will go to Theodoric's son. He will wish to thank me for saving the life of his father.'

'But *I* saved him!' Graham protested.

'On my orders.' Aetius smiled. 'Whatever the means, I have succeeded where the Tenctrama could not. And I must see to it that your friend the Doctor cannot aid Attila in the same way.'

Graham felt uneasy. 'What's that s'posed to mean?'

Aetius ignored him. 'Keep this man under guard in my quarters,' he told the centurion. 'Allow no one to see him.'

'We had a deal!' Graham called after him. 'I saved that bloke to make your alliance stronger. You said you'd help!'

But Aetius was gone. Graham's only answer was the prompting jab of the First Centurion's sword against his neck: 'Move.'

Chapter 19

In the alcove with Licinia, Ryan held his breath as a shadowy figure stepped cautiously into the Legion of Smoke's secret hall. Measured footsteps rang out on stone. The undersea lighting grew brighter.

'I'm exhausted,' came a deep voice, followed by the clatter of a helmet being slammed down on an altar. 'I fought three very strange Huns in a forest, I barely got away, I lost the target and my talk-box stopped working again. So don't jump out at me from your alcove, Liss, because I'm not in the mood.'

'It was his idea.' Liss shoved Ryan out of the alcove into the Hall, where he stumbled and almost fell flat on his face on the flagstones.

Ryan looked up to find a blond, attractive man in his late twenties staring down at him. 'Vitus, yeah?'

'That's right,' said Vitus, staring down at Ryan with fascination. He looked to be just the sort of guy Ryan had hated in school – built like a jock, but bright with it; the sort who made him feel clumsy and stupid. Being with the Doctor had shown him that some of that was just in his head, but it was easy to fall back into old ways of thinking.

'You said you lost the target – d'you mean Graham?' Ryan gave him a long look. 'Is he all right?'

'With dead Huns roaming the forest, I doubt it.'

'Spiritually dead?' Liss suggested, pouring liquid from a dusty flask into a small bowl. 'Dead at heart?'

'*Dead*, dead.' Vitus drained the bowl and smacked his lips. 'It's another one for the files, Liss.'

'What, that wine?'

He ignored her. 'I wanted you to come out and see them for yourself, but I can see you've been busy.' (Ryan suspected that Vitus's smile was mocking.) 'Has this one helped you with your enquiries?'

'And more.' She came up behind Ryan and stroked the back of his neck. 'You won't believe it, Vitus. Ryan came here in the TARDIS.'

Vitus snorted. 'That blue casket obsession of yours again?'

'The TARDIS really is a ship of space! Ryan knows the Doctor!'

'S'right.' Ryan felt self-conscious. 'We need to find her, and Yasmin and—'

'If you travel in a ship of space, you should be familiar with their machines.' Vitus held out a flat square of metal like Liss's talk-box. 'Why don't you fix it, Ryan?'

'You think there's, like, one firm supplying the whole universe?' Making a mental note to ask the Doctor about Apple products next time they were in the space year 17,000, Ryan studied the metal object, pressed the button on its side. Nothing happened, except that Vitus smirked. *I'll knock that smile off your face*, thought Ryan. With nothing to lose, he banged the talk-box on the altar three times. The blue glow flared into life. *In your face, Jock!*

'In the TARDIS we call these *communicators*,' he told Vitus, coolly handing it back. 'Now, want to hear what we think the Tenctrama are up to …?'

But Vitus wasn't listening, and neither was Liss. They were staring at the pulsating metal plate.

'The boss is calling,' Vitus said. 'He wants to talk.'

Yaz tried to walk as slowly as she could beside the Doctor, but their sweaty, sour-faced guards were having none of it, herding them along. The sky was still burning gold above them, weirding her out, and she felt sick at the thought of being held at knifepoint until the Doctor had presented Attila with his fully functional weapon of choice. While Yaz was to be taken to the Field of Shamans, the Doctor's workshop was to be set up in the tents of the Tenctrama, sited at the bounds of the camp.

'It's a good thing, really, Yaz, our splitting up.' The Doctor, as ever, was putting a positive spin on everything. 'I get to have a good poke around Inkri's lair, look for clues left behind about who the Tenctrama really are, where they've come from, what they're after. And you can get some rest.'

'I don't need any rest,' Yaz protested, but even as she spoke she felt dizzy. Her head was pounding, she hadn't slept in what felt like a week and she was still worried sick for Graham and Ryan. She was worried for everyone.

The higher land Attila had chosen for his tent gave a good view of the assembling armies. There was an impressiveness to the speed and precision of the parade as the soldiers filed into line, a grand scale to it all – it just seemed so terrible that the end result of all this was going to be a bloodbath.

They walked on through the vast camp, through blue smoke drifting from campfires, the smell of charcoal, meat and fat. Thirsty horses crowded at the dammed-off stream like aphids on a juicy vine, and servants hurried in all directions with jugs and kettles for their masters, or with sides of butchered meat draped over their backs. Their guards stopped to take the coconut half shells tied to their belts and dip them in a trough half full of water; green moss floated on the black surface like bacteria on a microscope slide, grossly enlarged. They offered one to the Doctor and Yaz. *Nice cup of cholera*, Yaz thought grimly, but she accepted all the same, parched as she was.

'This is where the shamans stay.' The stockier guard led them past a horse skull mounted on a tall pole that perhaps advertised wise men the way red-and-white stripes did a barber shop, and behind a line of wagons to where the shamans had pitched their tents; it gave the holy men some privacy as they went about their sacred work. The six tents, each covered with white horseskins, were arranged in a half-circle around a stone altar that bore the ashes of an old fire. No one was about.

'Thanks for dropping Yaz, Mr …? What's your name?'

He grunted. 'Bial.'

'Well, Bial, I bet the shamans had their noses put out of joint when the Tenctrama came along, eh?' The Doctor nudged him. 'You should tell them the hags have been booted out. They'll be back out here in no time, sharing the wisdom of your ancestors instead of sulking in their tents.'

Bial shook his head. 'The shamans *meditate*.'

'Meditation, right. Yeah, I pretend sulking is that, sometimes.'

Yaz smiled; she could hear the Shamans in their meditations now, quietly chanting inside their tents.

'I'd best be off!' the Doctor declared. 'Bye, Yaz. I'll be back as soon as I can. Oh, and Bial, I don't want a hair on her head harmed while I'm away, 'kay? Not a hair.' She rattled the sword hilt at her own guard's side. 'Come on then, march me faster …'

Bial glared at Yasmin and gestured that she should sit down on a bale of hay. She lay down on it instead and closed her eyes. She felt uneasy. The sky was still burning down above the plains of Catalaunum, and no one in Attila's camp knew why.

No one except for the creature watching from one of the tents, crouched over a shaman's muttering corpse.

The Doctor looked around the Tenctrama tent and sighed. The tent was made of bearskin. It was marked outside by a hank of long grey hair tied to a stake in the ground, and inside by the stink of smoke and rotting meat. The gloom was barely relieved by stubby candles. There was a rough-hewn workbench half buried with herbs and plants, a stone pestle and mortar, the bones of small animals, and wizened, shrivelled things that might once have been human heads, or possibly fruit with ideas above its station.

The guard, a charmer called Kason, hovered outside – he knew what Attila expected of him, but was clearly unhappy at being so close to the Tenctrama's inner sanctum. Just the effect, the Doctor supposed, that Inkri and her brethren would've been going for.

She leaned in closer to what looked to be the skull of a wild boar on a pedestal. 'See anything suspicious?' she asked, peering into its dark sockets.

Kason watched her sourly. She didn't judge; she suspected many Huns suffered stoically with resting bitch face. Instead she made him jump by sweeping away the foliage from the table.

'Set dressing!' the Doctor cried. 'Third-rate theatre to impress the likes of you! I mean, isn't this just exactly what you'd expect from a witch's lair? Props, aroma, colour scheme, it's perfect! But it has zero bearing on what's really been going on in here. N-O-W-T, nothing.'

'Work,' Kason hissed.

'Exactly, no sign of any real work being done at all.'

'*You* work.'

'Oh. Yes, I remember. Attila wants something horribly dangerous and destructive, doesn't he?' The Doctor leaned her elbows on the workbench. 'You know, a hero of mine once said that nothing in all the world is more dangerous than sincere ignorance and conscientious stupidity. So, as weapons go, Kason – how could I ever improve on you?'

'You work, or the brown-skinned woman will be killed.'

'See? Point proved.' The Doctor started pacing the tent. 'Is there a back way out of these things?'

'No.'

'Not one we can see, at least.' The Doctor pulled out the sonic. 'Unless, of course, we try looking very, very closely.'

Yaz drifted in and out of uneasy sleep. When she opened her eyes she found she was dazzled; the sky was still cocooning the Earth below with that golden glow. Looking away she realised that Bial – her Executioner-in-Waiting – had grown bored and given up. He was talking with another soldier, who was smearing his horse's nose in something dark.

'Where'd you get the blood, Chegge?' asked Bial. 'Rabbit?'

'Yeah, but it looks scary, right, Bial? Like he eats Romans.'

'Or like he ran into a tree.'

(Yaz thought she caught movement behind Chegge and Bial, just a glimpse. Wild white hair, a wrinkled face watching, hanging lopsided from shrunken shoulders; not Inkri, this one was somehow more revolting still. Yaz started, looked again, but saw only the soldiers.)

Bial held up a golden amulet on a chain around his neck. 'You should wear one of these. It has magical powers and will protect me.'

'Who says it'll protect you, your mother?'

'No,' laughed Bial. '*Your* mother, while she lay with me!'

(Yaz froze as the Tenctrama hag blinked into sight again, closer now, dressed in dark sackcloth rags and standing just behind Chegge. The shining eyes were fixed on Yaz. How could Bial not see her? There was a knife clutched in both of her claw-like hands. Yaz opened her mouth to call out a warning but no sound would come.)

Chegge had drawn his sword on Bial. 'Show me how your amulet will shield you from this blade, that has sent a hundred to their death!' But as he shouted, his horse whinnied and reared up, and snorted blood over his shoulders.

Bial only laughed. 'Perhaps I should trade in my amulet, eh, Chegge? Your horse protects me in its place!'

He was still laughing as the Tenctrama pushed the knife in his back. At the same time, she swept up her arm under Chegge's chin, and his head flew back with a crack of bones. Yaz tried again to shout out, both in horror and to raise alarm, as both men fell dead to the ground. The horse just stood there, dazed and forlorn with its bloodied muzzle. It took no notice of the Tenctrama that now stood beside it, advancing on Yaz with a gloating smile.

Keep away, Yaz wanted to scream, but the scream wouldn't come. She turned to run, but found men in ragged robes walking from the white tents with crimson throats, arms joined together to block her retreat, chanting softly over one another: 'All in the Pit, growing inside me, taken from the Pit, all from the Pit …'

Yaz turned again, saw the Tenctrama hag flicker in her vision. Suddenly the ancient woman was standing right in front of her, the lined, lopsided face up close and cackling. Yaz recoiled, rolled over the hay bale and started to run, circling behind the tents, aiming to get back to Attila's wooden palace. But another Tenctrama stepped out from between the tents, right in front of her.

It was Inkri.

Yaz tried to shove the old woman aside, but as she touched the old robes it was like they magnetised her to the scrawny form beneath. She couldn't pull away, couldn't shake herself free. Inkri's wrinkled fingers were digging into her own, the toothless smile became one of delight. Yaz felt the other hag place a hand on her shoulder, tangle her fingers in her hair. She caught cold breath on the back of her neck, a smell of decay that made her want to gag. The bony bodies pressed against her like two sides of a vice.

Then Inkri raised her dagger and thrust it down into the other crone's shoulder. For a confused moment, Yaz thought she was saved, that Inkri had had a change of heart. But a golden light enveloped her now, the glittering trails exploding outward, stretching up to the sky. Yaz looked down at her hands and saw they were transparent. She was fading away with the Tenctrama. *They don't die if you wound them*, Yaz realised, *it just releases some energy trapped inside.* But, energy for what?

'Doctor!' Yaz shouted, finding her voice at last, even as the hags' gurgling laughter drowned it out.

Chapter 20

The Doctor had made a study of the tent with the sonic. 'Found that back way we were talking about, Kason.'

The guard glowered and said nothing.

'Guess what? There's evidence of molecular excitation in the local area on multiple wavelengths. Or, in other words, a spell of teleportation. Perhaps the golden glow in the sky is evidence of the real Tenctrama lair, concealed up there among the clouds? It could operate the same way as a ceiling grid at the dodgems provides power to the vehicles below ...' She gasped, her voice rising with her enthusiasm. 'Yeah, vehicles. What if the Tenctrama are only vehicles for some kind of motivating force – an energy, or animus. Physical projections of an alien will.' She started dancing from foot to foot. 'Yeah, if you split open the flesh, the body unravels with the animus, and both are conducted back up to the Tenctrama ship, ready to be transported back down to Earth whenever! What do you reckon to *that*?'

'Work,' Kason said.

'Yes,' came a rasping whisper behind her. 'Work.'

The Doctor felt a sharp stab of foreboding and knew before she turned, from the sour, rotting stink in the air, that Inkri was back. Kason's resting bitch face was now a resting blank face; he showed no reaction at all – the same as Yaz and Attila in the war tent.

'By work, d'you mean the noble and exacting work of an unexpected escape?' The Doctor turned her sunniest face on the cadaverous crone. 'Thanks for switching off Kason, I'll be away now.'

Inkri seized her by the shoulder. 'You will stop seeking our secrets, Doctor. You will do as Attila asks, use your technology to make his weapons.'

'Of course, you're well up for that,' the Doctor said, 'cos it'll make the slaughter worse. Like you did when you separated Attila from his army and directed thousands more to their death going out in search of him. Why are you interfering in human wars? What do you stand to gain from this senseless killing?'

'Life,' Inkri hissed. 'The life of Yasmin Khan is now in our hands, not those of the Huns. And we will deliver on his threats so much more … unkindly than Attila ever could.'

The Doctor went cold to see Yasmin's pained and pleading expression staring out from the fire in the Tenctrama's ancient eyes. 'Let her go.'

Now the toothless smile returned. 'When you have finished your work.' With that, she crossed to Kason, who'd already drawn his sword. The Doctor looked away but heard Inkri's deranged screech as she exploded into vapour trails of light once more.

'Good getaway.' The Doctor checked the sonic with a smile. 'But maybe not as clean as you think.'

'Work,' said Kason, and the Doctor got busy doing just that.

Graham sat in Aetius's personal tent, still dressed in the big, fur robe, with his wrists tied. Watching over him was Consus the slave and between them both stood the big brass's big brass bathtub. What Graham wouldn't give for a good, hot soak right now! Well, perhaps after a change of water, which looked to be more of a soup of mud and blood. But since a bath was off the menu, what else could he do?

Escape, he told himself. With a big old battle ready to kick off, who would stop and question some well-to-do noble in fancy furs?

In the neighbouring tent, Aetius was having his conflab with King Theodoric, restored now and ready for active service. Voices were being raised.

'I am grateful for my life, Flavius Aetius,' Theodoric was saying, 'but you cannot ask us to cast out the Tenctrama as battle is about to begin!'

'I ask only that you forbid your witches from raising the dead to fight anew. Do they not serve their king …?'

Graham knew he needed to act before Aetius's discussion had ended. "Ere, Consus. Want me to get rid of that scar? I've got a bit left, I'd rather use it on you before your master nicks it.'

The slave looked unhappy, but nodded. 'Thank you.'

Graham fumbled inside the folds of his cloak for the pot of gel, listening to the diplomatic meeting.

'Our trenches mill with gibbering corpses,' Aetius proclaimed. 'What soldier will give his full life in battle knowing that *this* is his reward?'

'Let us hope some will,' said Theodoric, 'or else the Huns, dead or alive, will overrun us. Especially if Attila has found himself a new and stronger witch.'

'I have in my custody a man who knows Attila's new witch.' Aetius kept his voice strong and steady, keeping a lid on things. 'As the overtures of battle begin, my assassin will smuggle him into Attila's camp, where he shall lure out the witch to her death ...'

'Oh, no.' Graham felt his blood harden in his veins as the men went on talking. He found the pot of gel and pulled off the top. There were only smears left inside, but Consus didn't need to know that. 'Here you go.' He tossed the open pot into the bathwater. 'Oh, no! Rotten shot, sorry ...'

Graham got up slowly: this was the point in the plan where the slave would fish inside the tub for the miracle cure and, while distracted, Graham could push past him and make a break for it. Consus, though, just looked disappointed, staring glumly at the water.

'You, er, wanna fish that out, son?'

But the slave wasn't even looking at him. He was still gazing at the bath, his features slowly twisting in terror.

Graham looked too. 'Oh, my ...' The muddy, bloody water was churning; then suddenly, impossibly, the figure of a Tenctrama was rising from the tub; like he'd planted a magic bean in the water and this nightmare was growing from it. Gore and filth dripped from her matted hair and dribbled down her face as she stared at Graham, constellations of gold drifting in her dark eyes.

He managed to find his voice. 'Needed a bath, did you?'

Then he saw that she clutched the pot of gel between bony fingers; somehow, it had brought her here.

The crone put a fingertip to her lips as if to taste it. 'You bring science from distant stars,' came the chorus of voices. 'You wish to interfere with our rebirth.'

Graham shook his head. 'Not me, mate.'

She looked at Consus then recoiled from him and rounded on Graham. 'You are disruptive,' she hissed, 'and must be removed.'

She took a threatening step towards Graham through the water.

No, you don't! thought Graham. He rushed forward and tried to shoulder charge the witch, and get past her, but as he ran he tripped on a fold in the rug and headbutted the Tenctrama right in the face. There was a splintering noise as her nose caved in on itself, and a stinking dust flew up from her face. His knees struck the heavy brass tub, he fell and the crone tumbled out of the bath with him.

Graham landed on top of her. She writhed under him, mouth yawning open like the maw of some hideous beast as if to suck him inside. He felt her talons grip his back, start to sink into the flesh as she shook from side to side, panting and slobbering like a dog ...

Before he could even scream, Graham realised something was wrong. The Tenctrama's maggot-white skin was peeling and bubbling, her weird eyes scaling over, movements growing jerky. Graham pushed away from her, rolled clear as she shook like the lid on a pressure cooker and finally ignited into a storm of light and glittering dust.

He blinked in the aftermath, shocked and trying to process all that had just happened. But this was no time to look a wrinkled old gift-horse in its gaping mouth. The drone of voices in the war tent was humming on and Consus was just stood there, staring at the spot where the Tenctrama had been.

'Reckon I just saved your life, mate. You're welcome.' Graham quickly snatched the dagger from the slave's belt and held it out to him. 'Now, cut me loose, before another witch comes.'

Consus did as he was told, frantically sawing at Graham's ropes until they gave way. 'Now, I've got Aetius's robes.' Graham pulled the hood over his head to hide his face. 'The troops might just take me for Aetius off for a wander – if you're out there with me. You could lead me to the camp exit. What d'you think?'

Consus hesitated, took another lingering look at the dark, wet stains the Tenctrama had left behind on the rug. Then he nodded quickly. 'I'm deserting.'

'You and me both, kid.' Graham grinned and slapped him on the back. 'Nothing to lose but our chains, right?'

As they left the tent, Graham only wished that it was true.

Chapter 21

Yaz woke without opening her eyes. She could smell earth, and something rotting. For a horrible moment she thought she'd been buried alive, but no. There was dark space about her, and golden flecks like fireflies dancing in it …

With a gasp, Yaz tried to sit up but found she couldn't move. A Tenctrama was standing over her, eyes narrowed as if peering inside. 'The child carries no trace of our genetic modifications.'

'But she is human,' came the deep-high scratch of another Tenctrama voice. 'Her ancestors must have passed down the preparation.'

'No.' The crone-creature paused, then licked her lips. 'She shows no exposure to our treatments whatever.'

'The Doctor must possess the power to undo our work.'

'She does,' Yaz hissed.

The Tenctrama moved away, allowing Yaz a better look at her surroundings: it felt as if she were in a forest glade at night, surrounded by the stark shadows of dead trees. She was lying on a slab of stone that seemed to pulse with a slow heartbeat. It was cold. Hidden systems whirred and wailed around her.

'Is this your spaceship?' Yaz whispered.

'This is our haven,' came a familiar voice, as Inkri came out from the darkness. 'Anchored in the troposphere of this world until we finally gain what we need.'

'And what's that?'

'What we need to thrive through the centuries instead of merely endure them. And the Doctor will not stop us ...' The old crone hobbled closer, then stopped and screeched. 'Naelsa!'

The background rush of the haven's systems seemed to scream with her, shifting drunkenly between pitches.

'Naelsa is sick. Dying.' The other Tenctrama started to retch and shake. 'That trace of technology she detected in the Roman camp ...?'

'Poison.' Inkri looked straight up into the darkness. 'I don't understand ...'

'Reabsorption into the Pit has begun,' said the other. 'Her body will reform. She will tell us.'

'No, Enkalo!' Inkri was making shapes in the air over what looked to be an enormous, blackened tree stump. 'This poison will contaminate the Pit. There must be no reabsorption. Naelsa's remains must be vented. Vent her!'

Enkalo gripped a gnarled branch twisting out from another stump and heaved hard; the branch snapped in a cloud of golden spores. 'Naelsa endured for so long ... How did this happen?'

'Let us see.' Inkri's eyes looked wet as she straightened and crossed to some white vines like enormous maggots growing on the wall. She plucked strange fruit from among them: a slimy round crystal, into which she peered. 'Naelsa detected something unnatural in the Roman camp. She left her tent among the Visigoths to learn more and came in contact with an unknown regenerative agent.'

Sounds like the healing gel, Yaz realised.

'Naelsa told us the Visigoth king was brought back from the point of death.' She hissed like an angry snake. 'Some alien unguent?'

'Anyone tainted with this atrocity will be useless to us.'

'Tainted? It's medicine, healing gel – that's an atrocity to you?' But as Yaz spoke, she could see shapes and movement in the crystal: the little pot held in wrinkled fingers. Her heart banged harder as she recognised Graham – *You're alive!* He was staring in horror as if straight to camera; these had to be events from Naelsa's viewpoint, she realised, a record of her last moments. Graham hurled himself at Naelsa, there was a confused snatch of movement, a horrible scream …

Then the crystal cracked and crumbled in Inkri's hand. A single sparkling tear fell from her eye as she scattered the pieces on the floor. Was it sadness, wondered Yaz, or had Inkri felt the pain of Naelsa's death? The Tenctrama really were all linked in some way … but individuals could apparently be removed from the whole, their energy vented from the Pit.

'This healing gel your friend has used …' Inkri loomed over her. 'The Doctor made it?'

Enkalo came closer too. 'Is this how she cleansed your body of our mark?'

'I don't know what you're on about!'

'To undo what we have done to the humans, the Doctor must know of our plans.' Inkri placed a talon to Yaz's cheek. 'How? Where is she from?'

'Why do you interfere?' Enkalo added.

'We're just travellers.' Yaz tried to stay calm but could feel the Tenctrama trying to force their way into her thoughts. 'We came here in the TARDIS.'

'The blue box in the forest. It is a spaceship?'

'Kind of.'

Inkri hissed with impatience. 'The child knows too little.' She crossed to one of the dead trees and selected another crystal. This one shone a moving image from its depths, of the Doctor wandering round a tent with a goofy smile on her face, working the sonic and then studying the readings.

Yaz wanted more than anything just to reach out to her friend and see her again. 'Is that happening right now?'

'The Doctor must complete her work for Attila. The final irradiations have been made. She – and the genetic anomalies she has created – must be removed before the final death toll is achieved.'

'Why?' Yaz demanded. 'Why do you need so many people to die?'

'Why do you need them to live?' Inkri smiled slowly. 'We have given them purpose where, before, there was none.' She looked down at the crumbs of shattered crystal, Naelsa's last remains. 'Nothing lasts. Not in a single form. Certainly not your Doctor.'

'She must be watched constantly. She cannot be trusted.' Enkalo came to join her, carrying something like a dead rook in her hands. She placed the bird's body on a small stone pedestal, traced a pattern with her fingers on the side, and in a golden glow it disappeared. 'Now I will prepare Attila's shaman for his final performance.'

As Yaz watched, Enkalo shrank and shrivelled into the floor. She looked over at Inkri. 'How do you just live and die like that, but still remember who you are?'

'The fruit grows on the tree, it falls, it rots, its seeds grow again into new trees that will grow new fruits … An endless cycle.'

'Hate to break it to you, but you're not exactly peaches.'

'We are all projections from the Pit. And the Pit is so very, very old.'

'The dead down there,' Yaz said. 'They keep talking about the Pit. What is it – what are you planning to do to them?'

Inkri smiled and curled a talon through Yaz's hair. 'Soon we will be beautiful once again in our perfection.'

The Doctor loved building things, all kinds of things – from time-flow analogues out of kitchen bits to dry stone walls, from Arthur C. Clarke's designs for a digital lawnmower to proper challenges like assembling flatpacked Ikea wardrobes. She didn't normally mind being watched – what good was being brilliant if you had no one to boggle and applaud? – but the dead crow eyeing her coldly from its perch on the table beside her was putting her off her game. Golden skeins flitted across the dark, beady eyes: eyes of the Tenctrama.

'Give the poor thing some dignity, let her go,' the Doctor said, staring straight into the crow's head. 'You can see I'm recharging the force-field generator.' She buzzed again with the sonic, checked the reading. 'You know what it can do, Attila knows what it can do.'

The crow's eyes blinked, and it edged its head to one side.

'When it's ready,' she went on, 'I'll tell you and then, *then* – you bring Yasmin back to me safe and sound and I'll hand it over, just as you want. Otherwise, I'll smash it.'

The crow held silent and still. Then it pushed out its wings and flew up at the Doctor's face. She recoiled and it flapped past, hit the canvas wall and fell in a heap on top of the other dead birds the Tenctrama had sent to spy on her.

'I'm so sorry,' she murmured, crossing to the crow and stroking its burning hot head. The optic link blazed through their little brains, they couldn't last long. The Doctor swallowed back her anger – there would be a time for anger, soon – flicked on the sonic, and returned to the jobs in hand.

The job the Tenctrama thought she was doing on the force-field generator, and the job she prayed would save Yaz's life.

Attila had summoned his council of war, the elder chieftains and nobles of many of the various tribes fighting under his banners. What a stink of colour and opinion they brought to his tent! But the talk, the camaraderie, the sheer presence of so many seasoned warlords gathered around the same table in another land, quickened the blood, told all present that glorious battle was pressing upon them. Since, in times of change, tradition steadied soldiers, to consolidate support and show he had broken faith with the Tenctrama, Attila had summoned Shallo, the wisest of his old shamans, to address the council with good augurs, to boost morale still further.

'It is good to see wise men in place of witches,' Chokona said, to much approval around the table. 'We spent too long in their company.'

Attila ignored the implied criticism. In the council, everyone had a chance to voice his mind freely. The chieftains would, he knew, fight better if they felt their beliefs and opinions respected.

Shallo moved more stiffly than Attila remembered, but then he had been left out in the cold of ill-favour for two years or more. When you tried on old boots the leather took time to bend comfortably again. The old shaman's skin was stretched tight over his bones, and a jackdaw sat upon the back of his neck, peeping about from behind his bald, scarred head, lending him an air of power and mystery.

'We have inspected the entrails of cattle,' Shallo said. 'We have scraped the bones and distinguished the path of the beasts' veins. All point alike.'

Attila nodded, indulging the old man his theatre. 'And to what do they point?'

The shaman paused, closed his eyes. He began to sway.

Chokona stared, rapt. 'He is communing with the spirits.'

The jackdaw gave a throaty call as if in agreement, or to call Shallo back.

Attila tired of the show. 'Speak plainly to your king.'

The shaman's eyes snapped open and his voice was a low whisper. 'The Hun dead will stay dead. But the Romans who fall will rise again.' He looked round the table as if seeking support. 'You must release the Strava from their cages to feast on the flesh of our enemies.'

A low murmur of unease ran around the table.

'The Tenctrama gave us words to command the Strava,' Chokona said, 'to make them attack and kill. But now the hags are dead, will their beasts stay under our control?'

'They will,' Shallo said.

Attila was surprised his shaman would embrace the legacy of the Tenctrama, but also pleased; he smarted still from the Romans unleashing their own beast at the Aube, and wished them to feel teeth in return. 'Victory will be ours if we unleash the Strava?'

'Of course.' Shallo bowed stiffly from the waist. 'A gift given by one we detest is still a gift.'

Lasett, the Sarguri chieftain, drank deeply from a bowl of horse blood, which to her seemed sweet as wine. 'The beasts will help us to take the hill,' she said. 'Let them match our ferocity as we fight.'

Chokona nodded. 'And let Aetius and his army endure only in the bellies of our dogs!'

'It is agreed, then.' Attila knew when to smile and when to bring down the boot, and his decision in matters of war was final. 'We will let loose the Strava as we take the hill.'

Assent was hesitant at first, but then the banging of golden goblets on the table began and oaths were sworn. Attila smiled and sipped from his plain wooden bowl. He cared nothing for the trappings of wealth, only the power and fealty that it could command. And once he had the Doctor's crystal wand in his hand, its power would make all people fear him in the same way they feared the Tenctrama. One day, he would command the whole world.

'The Doctor's work goes well?' he asked Shallo.

Shallo nodded again. 'We hold the young witch in our tents. Her power shall be yours.'

'One power among so many,' said Attila, smiling around at his chieftains; though inside he was warmed by Shallo's words, he knew he could not be seen to be dependent on anyone or anything. 'Now, to summarise: when battle commences—'

'You'll have this.'

The room fell silent as the Doctor entered the tent with her guard. She looked tired and drawn, smudges of dirt over her pale complexion. Attila's heart quickened to see that in her hand, she held the crystal stick with which he had torn trees from the forest. 'You have done as I ordered.'

'Obviously,' the Doctor said with an affable grin. 'Are you not my lord Attila? Do I not tremble at your every command? Do I not lay it on thick enough, O great master?'

Attila's eyes flashed warning as he rose from his great chair. 'Remember Yasmin. She is in my hands.'

'So you tell me.' The Doctor regarded Shallo. 'Hello. You look dead on your feet. Here to reassure folks the old ways are back?'

Shallo glared back coldly. 'The Doctor's weapon will win us this battle.'

'For me, there is *no* way to win this battle,' the Doctor said. 'But I've done what you want. I've found a way to project the power of the force-field generator, over distance and … well, anyway, fancy a demo? I've laid on some wagons. Well, not literally. I've set up some wagons for target practice. Shall we …?'

Attila strutted after her and saw that three armoured wagons had been moved into position some way off at the bottom of the rise. An arrow shot from here would most likely bounce off the steel sides. But now the Doctor handed him the glowing stick. It had a black wire looped around its base like a hilt, and a small ball of metal placed in an indentation. 'I gave it a button,' she said. 'Point and shoot. But choose the moment carefully, because once you've fired, it'll need a few minutes to recharge …'

Attila was not listening. He pointed the crystal rod at the middle of the wagons and pressed on the metal. With a groan that was almost too low to be heard, the rod lit up red and then the wagons were struck by invisible lightning: shattered, scattered, thrown over like a child's toys.

For a few seconds, all was silent. Then cheers went up from the chieftains, fists of defiance were brandished at the Roman forces still gathering in the distance. Attila turned and smiled, graciously acknowledging his generals' love for him, and raised his weapon aloft. 'Only Attila has this power!' he shouted. 'The armies of Rome will not hold with their centres devastated by *my* magicks …'

Attila didn't need to go on; the loud assents were drowning him out. Why, he could win this war single-handed now!

'I've done what you want,' said the Doctor, and she turned from Attila to address the jackdaw on Shallo's shoulder. 'Now, take me to my friend.'

'Do it,' said Attila. 'I have war to make.'

The shaman smiled and turned to lead the Doctor away, beginning to babble once more under his breath, over and over: 'Together in the Pit, all rising from the heart of the Pit to walk strong again together in the Pit, the great Pit …'

The Doctor nudged the jackdaw aside and saw the sticky wound left by the Tenctrama knife that had severed Shallo's brainstem. She stopped walking for a few moments, bunched her fists.

Then she quickened her step.

Chapter 22

Graham kept his head down and kept walking through the Roman camp. Soldiers saluted him as he passed – with Consus by his side, people must assume that the *Magister Militum* and his servant were inspecting the camp … at least he hoped they did.

His luck held until he neared one of the guarded checkpoints at the perimeter. So far, marching past with his eyes on the ground and a wave of the hand had worked pretty well, but suddenly he heard ahead of him – 'Flavius Aetius, sir!' The voice rang clear as a bell. 'I urge you to receive my most urgent report.'

Marvellous, thought Graham. 'Er, not now,' he said, trying to mimic the deep, dry tones of Aetius. 'Busy. Slave. Walk.'

'Wait. Sir?'

Graham raised his head a little, saw a black horse canter towards him, someone in armour riding on its back, fingers at the hilt of the long sword by his side.

It was Vitus, from the Legion of Smoke. He looked up a little further and saw the young man's face, soft and clear and framed with short blond hair. Clearly Vitus had not joined the dead after all, following his run-in with the zombie Huns in the woods. But Graham didn't feel so clever now about his own chances of staying alive …

'Ah, most gracious patrician Flavius Aetius, perhaps you will allow me to travel with you as you venture forth,' Vitus went on. 'For the woods are not safe. There are all kinds of spectres lurking there.'

'No, you're all right.' Graham waved the arm again.

'Some talk of a black man who casts bright light from his hand, dazzling those who might bring him and his elder compatriot down.'

Graham stopped so abruptly that Consus banged into him. Elder compatriot? Vitus clearly knew he was addressing Graham, not Aetius, and yet wasn't dropping him in it.

'Stand down the barriers, you men,' Vitus went on, 'else Flavius Aetius will flog you!'

'Damn right I will,' said Graham. Up ahead, he could hear the sound of low conversations, barricades being hastily dismantled, the creak of heavy carts as they were pushed aside. *Righty-ho, then.* He walked on by, Consus at his side, with the clip-clop of Vitus's horse just behind him.

The walk seemed to last for ever but finally he heard the slave's steady footsteps break away as the boy ran for it without another word.

'I'm guessing we're round the bend, then …?' Graham pulled back the heavy woollen cloak from his head and turned to face Vitus. 'I *must* be round the bend, trusting you. How come you helped me?'

'Because time is short, Graham O'Brien,' said Vitus.

'What're you playing at? Why'd you turn up at the camp and then turn round again? Have you seen Ryan?'

Vitus just looked at him, grinning. 'Yes, I have seen Ryan. He is well, and with my associate in the Legion of Smoke.'

'He's all right? You mean it?' Graham felt about two feet taller. 'Can you take me to him? Somehow we've got to find the Doctor and Yaz – our two friends, I mean – in the Hun camp. Aetius was calling in some assassin to take me there and force me to bring out the Doctor so he could murder her …'

Graham trailed off. Vitus had pulled a flat, grey disc from inside his tunic and placed it to the side of his temple. 'Sir, this is Vitus. Don't worry about your missing prisoner, I've got him here with me. We will proceed together to the Hun camp as agreed.'

Aetius's voice crackled from the disc. 'Good. Move, then, and quickly.' There was an electronic squawk and the disc fell silent.

'*You're* the assassin,' Graham said dully. 'With an ancient Roman communicator?'

'We'll talk as we go,' Vitus told him, putting the communicator away. 'I think we both have some catching up to do.'

The Doctor followed Shallo through the near-deserted camp. The men making ready for war were gone; they'd emerged now, from their chrysalises of leather and iron, as soldiers. The blacksmiths, the arrow-makers, the cooks and servants, the lifeblood of the camp, had left their posts and gathered on the high ground, staring down at the battlefield as the two gigantic armies, hundreds and thousands of men, faced each other over the plain in eerie silence, each second stretching out for an eternity.

Shallo stopped by a makeshift stable that was more like a lean-to and just stood there, muttering. The Doctor smiled as she recognised one of the horses standing just inside. 'Bittenmane!' He came out to see her, snorted and pressed his head against her shoulder. 'Hello, boy. I won't ask why the long face, because we both know you're a horse.' She patted his right flank. 'Cuts and grazes all healed up, though! I'm glad Attila let you rest for a bit. You've been through a lot. Just like … Yaz!' The Doctor looked up in delight as she saw Yaz stagger forward from behind the stables. 'Oh, Yaz! I've been so worried.'

'Doctor,' she said, slurring the words. 'Watch out, they're not … letting us …'

'Go?' The Doctor nodded as Yaz's eyes closed and Inkri and Enkalo stepped out from behind her. 'Yeah, I sort of thought that might happen. Honestly, you alien invaders! You say one thing and do another. I notice this, in my line of work.'

'And your work is protecting the people of Earth?' Inkri's voice was cold. 'Other space powers have come here.'

'I remember a couple of them.'

'We used our powers to preserve humanity.'

'The way a hungry woman preserves her dinner?' The Doctor looked steadily into those old, half-watt eyes. 'You're not invaders, are you? You're more like farmers. How long have you lingered on this planet now?'

'The process of renewal can take over a thousand years,' said Enkalo, hovering beside Yaz. 'The ground must be prepared before the seeds can be planted.'

'And you're not just speaking metaphorically, are you?' The Doctor frowned, wondering aloud. 'A process of renewal; a thousand years preparing the ground for the Tenctrama seed. And the ground is humanity.'

'*All* animal life shall be harvested,' Inkri informed her. 'We have spent so long inculcating our seed within the proteins and enzymes of living things, over so many generations.'

'Introduced your own essence to their food and drink. Irradiated them with your sky-fire and left them to simmer. Now they're *al dente* and good to go as a nourishing meal.' The Doctor looked over as some kitchen boys approached, glazed over, turned and walked away; the Tenctrama were keeping this meeting private. 'How do you collect that nourishment?'

'We must gather from the fresh dead. Death in volume is needed.'

'You hearing this, bestie?' the Doctor called over to Yaz, whose eyes were still shut. 'Explains why the Tenctrama have been manipulating the barbarian kings – the movers and shakers who can bring this world to war.' Now she turned the full force of her glare on Inkri. 'The ones who can provide them with "the fresh dead" on an obscene scale.'

'You talk to us of scale in war?' said Inkri. 'Our ancestors all but destroyed themselves with the most terrible weapons. Weapons that distorted life to such a degree—'

'That you were the end result?' The Doctor nodded sadly. 'A handful of survivors, parasitic vampires, haunting the battlegrounds, leeching from the dead.'

'Survival gave us hunger,' said Enkalo. 'Hunger gives us purpose. We drift through space in search of stock. We target animals who can shape their environment and splice our DNA with theirs, disguise ourselves, move among them, prepare the ground …'

'Finally,' said Inkri, 'we harvest.'

'Not here you don't,' the Doctor snapped. 'How many billions have died already to sustain the Tenctrama? How many worlds left dead behind you?'

'We do not take *all* life from any world. If the population recovers, there will be more harvests in years to come.'

'Wait. You're not just answering questions, you're volunteering information. Now I'm wondering why.'

'Because outrage and anger are such visceral feelings.' Inkri smiled. 'They distract your mind from what's actually happening.'

'Oh …' With a surge of dismay, the Doctor found she couldn't move. There were gold flickers speckling her sight. She'd let these creatures worm their fingers inside her mind, and now pain knifed through her. 'What … what are you doing?'

'Killing you. You, and those you have despoiled, must be removed before the harvest can begin.'

Inkri hobbled closer. The Doctor cried out as pain and pressure built up inside her head. Her vision began to blur but she could not blink. Inkri's fingertips pressed against her temples and began to burn.

Chapter 23

The Doctor gasped, and Inkri's face bobbed closer. She whispered, 'Are you going to scream, Doctor?'

'I'm ... going to ... *whistle*.'

She turned to Bittenmane and blew through her teeth, the same notes she'd heard often around the camp. Bittenmane darted forward, between the Doctor and Inkri, knocking the crone backwards, breaking the contact. Movement surged back into the Doctor's limbs with a tsunami of pins and needles. As Bittenmane passed, the Doctor lurched after him, grabbed hold of his shaggy mane and heaved herself onto his back.

'That Bittenmane, eh, Inkri? Bit of a dark horse ...' As she landed in the saddle and dug her heels into his sides to drive him onward, the Doctor saw the banner of a sickle moon shift suddenly upward at the forefront of the Hun forces. A clear signal from Attila's forces – but for what?

Inkri rose from the ground, leathery face twisting in rage as she pointed at Yaz. 'Destroy her, Enkalo!'

Bittenmane flattened his ears to his head, running like he was in the front line as the Doctor steered him round in a circle. Enkalo had turned to Yaz, hands reaching for her face. But the Doctor rode up behind her and barged her aside, sending her old bony body rolling over in the dirt.

'Yaz!' The Doctor shouted, bringing Bittenmane to a stop beside her friend. She knew she didn't have long, that the Tenctrama would soon recover.

Then a wave of noise shattered through the Hun camp, as the bugler on the ramparts of Attila's wooden palace blasted the great ivory battle-horn. The rising note was insanely loud, like a shudder from hell. Its message was deafening, a clear answer to the signal from the battlefield.

'Time to take the hill,' the Doctor breathed.

Graham wasn't happy about many things as Vitus guided their horse through the precarious scrub that bordered the Hun camp. He wasn't happy that he was holding on tight to an assassin with orders to kill his mates. He wasn't happy that the man smelled like he hadn't had a bath in months. He wasn't happy that they were somehow supposed to get inside the Hun camp in one piece, and he definitely wasn't happy when the pug-ugly Hun scout rose up from the bushes just ahead of them with a dirty great bow and arrow.

Two more jumped up from the ground with swords at the ready. Graham was about to swear loudly; if you couldn't let loose a bit of Anglo-Saxon in this time, well ...

But then unexpected sci-fi sounds cut through the air. Vitus had some sort of space gun in his hand! The two attacking Huns fell in quick succession, smoke belching from their chests. At the same time the bowman loosed his arrow, but Vitus had forced his horse hard left and the missile whooshed past. One more blast from the laser gun, and the archer fell back in a cloud of dust.

'What the hell!' Graham spluttered.

Vitus held up the white ceramic pistol. 'They do not have this technology where you are from?'

'No! Where'd you get it?'

'It was found centuries ago in a mine in Africa, beside the ancient remains of a beast unknown on this world.'

Graham supposed the twenty-first century didn't have a monopoly on alien invasions; Earth must always have looked a juicy proposition to E.T. eyes. 'So the Legion was still going centuries back – and they pinched this gun?'

'They stopped it falling into the wrong hands.' Vitus sighed. 'Can you imagine if men gained the power to wipe out whole empires with a single strike? Can you imagine the desperate danger that would come with possessing such weapons?'

'Yeah,' Graham said. 'I think I can.'

Vitus held up a hand to silence him as a familiar muttering started up: 'All in the Pit, made whole in the Pit, come out from the Pit …' The Huns were getting up, the blood from their wounds hardening, flesh filling out from within like rising bread.

'Come on, Ke-mo Sah-bee.' Graham kept patting Vitus on the shoulder. 'Get us out of here!'

As they reached the end of the scrubby tree line, the gateway to the Hun camp stood only two hundred metres off. 'Might as well be miles away,' Graham murmured, 'for all the chance we have of getting in.' A small town had been dragged into the outer defences of the place, with guards holding javelins and scythes and armoured wagons standing in front and giant cages that held ... Whoa, what the hell were those things?

The long, ominous note of a horn thrummed through the camp. Graham felt dread, deep and primal, prickling its way through his chest. It was a call to arms, loud enough to ...

Wake the dead.

The after-echo of the bugler's signal rolled out along the fields. Still balanced on Bittenmane's back, stretching awkwardly to clutch Yaz about the shoulders, the Doctor pulled out the sonic as a hair-raising chorus of shouts and battle cries went up from the battlefield.

A ghastlier war cry went up from closer by as Inkri came hovering through the air towards them, mouth wide open in a deformed grin, golden energy sizzling between the rigid claws of her hands, ready to unleash hell.

'Here goes everything,' the Doctor muttered. Pulling Yaz in for a tighter hug, she twisted on the sonic with her spare hand.

And the Doctor, Yaz and Bittenmane disappeared.

On higher ground within the camp, smiths and servants watched tensely as the eerie calm across the battlefield broke hard when the left flank of Attila's army poured forward. Thousands of Huns on horseback raced away pursued by a vast swathe of allied warriors armed with scythes and javelins, whips, bows and arrows, hatchets, daggers ...

Bittenmane glowed back into being just in front of the crowd, the Doctor still on his back, Yaz pressed up against them both. The Huns scattered in panic at this unearthly visitation, all except one burly smith who stayed rooted to the spot.

'Pardon my witchcraft! Not staying long. I hope.' The Doctor was losing her grip on Yaz, who was sinking to her knees. 'Quickly! You!' She pointed to the smith. 'Help my friend onto the horse, will you? She's a witch's familiar, but really ever so nice!'

The smith picked up Yaz, almost threw her onto the back of the horse, and then ran.

'Can't say I blame you.' The Doctor turned back to Yaz, whose eyes were flicking open. 'Hey,' she said, searching out her friend's face. 'You back with me? The jump away from the Tenctrama should've shaken their mental hold …'

'Yeah.' Yaz licked dry lips. 'What happened?'

'I'm in the middle of a daring rescue attempt.'

'Are you smashing it?'

'Well, I've hacked into the Tenctrama teleport field, but the sonic can only simulate the energy wavelengths and the transport receptors aren't fooled for long. Short hops only in random directions—'

'Let's say you're smashing it.'

'Yaz, I'm totally smashing it! Now, hold on tight.' The Doctor felt Yaz's arms lock around her waist. She whistled again, and Bittenmane reared up, hooves flailing. 'Once more into the breach, dear friend!'

*

Legionaries Zeno and Ricimer heard the horn's low warning clear across the plains. They were standing guard on the ridge of land in between the two defensive trenches at the front of the camp. Both trenches were filled with the muttering dead from the skirmish at the Aube, stumbling over the wooden stakes arranged so as to impale anyone unwise enough to try leaping across.

'That's the Huns' alarm call,' said Ricimer.

Zeno watched through clouds of dust as a body of Rome's allied forces, led by Theodoric the Visigoth, responded to the rallying call and tore away to meet the oncoming Huns. 'There goes the miracle man. S'pose Aetius thinks Theodoric's amazing recovery will inspire the troops.'

'He's probably right.' Ricimer nodded to the twitching bodies in the trenches. 'It'll give them hope they won't all come back like these poor sods.'

'Thank God we're too vital to the defence of the camp to participate in the assault, eh?'

'Irreplaceable. That's us, Zeno.'

The two men shared a look and then a laugh. Then they heard shouts from their fellow guards along the defensive line.

Zeno's flesh crawled to see that the dead had suddenly started climbing out from both trenches. They were digging their fingers into the muddy slopes, hauling themselves up and over the edge; those at the front were staggering jerkily away after the troops assigned to battle, while those from the inner ditch tried to leap across the second, landing on those who were already climbing and grabbing hold, trampling each other in their blind haste to join in the action.

'What the …?' Ricimer looked helplessly at Zeno as the inner trench kept disgorging the whispering, patch-faced corpses. 'Should we be stopping them?'

'Stuff that,' said Zeno, standing aside as a centurion in filthy, bloodied dress barged past. 'If they want to go, let them—'

He never finished. A dead soldier walked into him, and he toppled over into the outer trench. Before Ricimer could even shout in warning, he'd heard the *thunk*, shriek and scrape of a man who'd met the sharp end of a big stick. Heart sinking, Ricimer peered over the edge, saw Zeno flailing weakly in a pit of unbothered bodies, cradling the post protruding from his belly. His head fell back, and bounced against the mud.

Ricimer waited, everything held clenched, waiting for Zeno to raise his head, calm and muttering, for the blood to dry around the wound even as he got back up, the stake stuffed through him like he was a rabbit on a spit. But it didn't happen. Zeno twitched twice and then just lay there.

'Thank God.' Ricimer felt a tear roll down his cheek, one of relief as much as sadness. 'Whatever else comes, this nightmare of the dead rising has ended.'

But as he watched, a glowing apparition rose up from the trench beside Zeno's body, a hideous hag in sackcloth rags, hissing with rage, thin white hair floating around her lopsided face. 'The tainted cannot rise. The tainted cannot be taken.' So saying, she bent over Zeno and dug her clawed fingers into his temples. Ricimer stared, horrified, as golden energy coursed through Zeno, engulfed him until he looked like an effigy blackening in impossible flames, while the oaken spike that had killed him stood untouched.

A choked sob escaped Ricimer's lips. The vision of the hag heard and looked up, and her toothless smile grew wide.

'One out, one in,' she said.

Then she rose up, shrieking, and gripped Ricimer by the throat. A split second later he was thrown down into the trench and impaled on the same stake, straight through the heart. Death was instant. Ricimer felt nothing. He didn't feel his eyes snapping back open, or his hands twitch as they pulled at the blood-slick stake. Didn't flinch as flesh bubbled out from inside him to seal the gaping hole. His tongue tugged at the words trapped in his head like angry wasps – *'caught in the Pit, all of us, reborn in the Pit'* – as he climbed out of the trench with all the others and stumbled past the gloating hag, ready to kill every stinking Hun on the plains of Catalaunum.

Graham covered his ears as fifes, horns and drums rose up and answered the bugle's challenge before they too were eclipsed by the cheers of men in their thousands. It made fifty thousand footie fans at the London Stadium sound like a kids' birthday party.

A massive cage close by to the entrance was thrown open and a colossal beast came stampeding out. Spiky and furry with snapping jaws crammed with teeth, it looked like a wolf had grown to the size of a family car and swallowed a rhino. More of the cages, studding the long defensive line into the distance, were being opened up and identical creatures came bounding out on warped, misshapen limbs, each studded with claws like thorns on the branch of a giant rose bush. The creatures were making for the hill, and they were pursued by an army of disfigured men, shambling out from the town building in a horrible flood: faces blank, limbs twitching but still clutching swords and axes, whips and daggers, clothes and helmets torn and bloody but the flesh behind bunged with puckered pink, like the skin beneath a wet blister. They smashed through the checkpoint, trampling Hun guards in their way.

Graham felt sick; he didn't want to watch, but couldn't tear his eyes away from the spectacle. There was a war going on, and these running dead were going to join it in their hundreds, no, *thousands* … Graham just sat there on the back of the horse, gaping, struggling to grasp how so many people could've been cut down and killed and still leave so many behind. The worst that could happen to these boys had already happened, and now they looked set to drag after them anyone they could.

The Doctor set off at a fast gallop back down the hill into the heart of the Hun camp, Yaz holding on for dear life. Inkri and Enkalo glowed into existence just a few metres in front of them.

With a further twist of the sonic, the Doctor, Yaz and their mount glowed back out of it, fading away. 'Not today, thank you …!'

*

171

Graham jumped at a noise behind him. The border guards that Vitus had killed had given up on the chase and instead were hacking their way out through the scrub; summoned by the call to arms, they charged after the legions of the dead already piling towards the hill that Romans and Huns alike had made their target.

'Why hunt and kill two of the enemy,' said Vitus, 'when you can run straight into two hundred?'

'Quantity over quality,' Graham agreed, staring out at the swarms moving from both sides across the battlefield. There were so many that individual men and horses became just a roiling mass of sheer aggression.

And then he gasped so hard he coughed, and his body shook.

'Oh, my gawd.' He pointed. 'Never mind getting into camp – look at that. The Doctor and Yaz already got out!'

Vitus's bushy brows angled upward. 'And it looks like they'll do my job for me.'

Bittenmane galloped the Doctor and Yaz back into existence on the plain. 'Yee-hah!' the Doctor shouted. 'That's more like it. We've jumped clear out of the camp!'

'More like it?' Yaz clung on, gazing around wildly. 'Look!'

The two opposing armies, a vast swathe of Huns to the right and Romans to the left, were closing in on them from either side.

Yaz swore. 'We've come out in the middle of the battlefield!'

Chapter 24

Bittenmane was speeding like a dark rocket, halfway along the high ridge of land that was the only tactical standout on the plain. To their right, Yaz saw that Attila's combined forces – with several of the Strava out in front like tusked, hairy juggernauts – were closing on them fast.

Yaz clung on tighter. 'Why does everyone care about this stupid hill so much?'

'High ground makes it harder for the enemy to out-flank you.' Just as the Doctor spoke, the Roman hordes swarmed over the top of the hill, three of their own Strava leading the charge. The Doctor had to shout over the pounding of hooves and claws and the shouts of the soldiers which left the whole world shaking around them. 'Mounts and monsters move faster downhill, while arrows strike harder, so possession of the hill could prove decisive …'

'For someone who hates war you know a lot about it!'

'Never hate something until you understand it.'

Yaz yelled, 'I hate that we can't teleport out of here!'

'Trying.' The Doctor veered away from the Romans, kept flicking the sonic on and off, but nothing was happening. 'It's no good! Inkri's shut me out of the transmitter system.'

'Boost the power?'

'Gee-up, Bittenmane!' The Doctor leaned forward in the saddle. 'Horsepower is all we've got!'

The Hunnic forces were barely a thousand metres from Bittenmane – and closing fast. Yaz felt the endless jolt and thump of the earth under Bittenmane's hooves, her hearing crushed by the clamour of the approaching armies, her vision corkscrewing between unsteady flashes of men and monsters drawing near on both sides. There was no way to outrun the clash of armies, no way to escape the twin tsunamis about to break over them. She gripped the Doctor tightly enough to break her in half. 'Doctor, I'm sorry.'

'Sorry?' the Doctor shouted back. 'What for?'

'If I hadn't been caught, you wouldn't have had to rescue me and—'

'Don't talk like it's all over, Yaz.' The sonic was back in her hand. 'I gave Attila a super-weapon, just like the Tenctrama asked!'

'You did *what*?'

'That was the deal in exchange for your life. Anyway, he's bound to use it. And when he's in range … assuming my lash-up has held …'

Yaz couldn't even hear her any more. The assault on her senses was too much. Rolling to their right, the Hun avalanche was set to engulf them, barely a hundred metres away. *This is where it ends*, she thought, water whipped from her eyes by the wind as they galloped on, *but I'm not going to die crying, I'm just going to hold on to the Doctor and ...*

A prickling heat radiated from her right. All she could hear was the buzz of the sonic; it was like the sound had been sucked from her ears. Yaz risked opening her eyes, and then risked them popping out at the sight that awaited her.

It looked as if the Strava had ridden into a wall of invisible gum, as if the air itself was stretching, slowing them down. Hun riders behind them in the ranks, unable to stop in time, slammed into them. Soon, horses crammed against horses, pushing those in front up against the solid air, close enough almost to stab at the Doctor and Yaz as they rode by. Yaz saw the dog-bitten faces of those Hun warriors screwed up in pain and anger as they struggled against this pliable but apparently impenetrable barrier. Behind them to their left, the Roman forces rode full-pelt into the same invisible barricade some fifty metres deep with the same inevitable effect. Horses and riders were rammed into a struggling mass of limbs. A Strava with grey, matted fur, scythe-like claws and tusks like a woolly mammoth on steroids was tearing at the air, desperate to get to the confused huddle of Huns so close, yet impossibly out of reach.

Senses stunned, Yaz's mind still fought to figure it out: 'You gave Attila the force-field generator?'

'Once I'd made a few adjustments,' the Doctor agreed, urging Bittenmane onward. 'Like, leaving it with enough charge for just one more shot, and softening the field density. Instead of projecting a hammer-hard wall of air, it spat out a big squishy barrier. With the sonic disrupting the energy field, we can carve a path through it – it'll be like galloping inside a giant invisible bubble.'

'So the two sides can't fight!' A nasty thought struck Yaz. 'Until the bubble goes pop.'

'That's right. And I'm afraid we're weakening it all the time just by riding through it.'

Bittenmane whinnied as the side of his head struck something invisible, lurched and almost lost his footing.

'Structure's breaking down already!' The Doctor whistled and Bittenmane compensated, veering right, terrifyingly close to the Hun army and the horrifying maw of a slavering Strava. Yaz felt her leg burn as they brushed its inside edge, and Bittenmane whinnied with terror. Behind them, she saw the Roman forces suddenly surging forward deeper into the weakening barrier, falling over each other. Men and beasts alike were being trampled, on the Huns' side too.

Feeling sick, Yaz pressed her face against the Doctor's back. There was no miracle solution, no magic way to stop the fighting and avert the casualties. All the Doctor could do was hope not to make it worse – and stay alive long enough to fight back against the Tenctrama.

'Almost there.' The Doctor spoke encouragement to Bittenmane through gritted teeth. 'Come on, boy, just a little further …'

Finally Yaz felt the air clearing around them. Bittenmane shook his head and reared up, almost throwing his riders, until the Doctor gave a sharp whistled signal and the horse recovered himself. Yaz realised that she was panting for breath, that her clothes were clinging to her back with sweat – and that, somehow, she was still alive! And all this while, behind them, the forces of Rome and Attila were charging at each other in slow motion, falling and tumbling in a surreal nightmare of acrobatics.

'We must get clear of the battlefield,' the Doctor said, pricking Bittenmane's sides once more.

'And go where?'

'Um ... how about towards Ryan and that nice-looking lady knight over there?'

'What?' Yaz looked up, astonished, and saw the two figures in the distance, one darker, jumping up and down and waving his hands. 'That *is* Ryan! Where'd he spring from?'

'I have no idea!' The Doctor stood up in the saddle and waved back madly. 'Let's go and find out!'

'Oh, my days!' Ryan shouted. 'There they are! They're all right! They're alive!'

'And look at the battle!' Liss's eyes were copying her mouth, stretched wide open. 'It's impossible. How in Hades did she part the ways between two clashing armies?'

'Course it's impossible. She's the Doctor, isn't she?'

Ryan turned to check he hadn't lost their exit back to the catacombs; it was little more than a burrow at the foot of a small hillock and not easy to spot. The last section of their long journey through the miles of underground catacombs had seen them down on hands and knees through a tiny passage off the main tunnel; the excavators had most likely dug it for ventilation as they worked.

'Come on, Doctor …' She was still riding that shaggy old horse towards them. He felt exposed enough standing just here, how must she and Yaz feel? Ryan kept nervous eyes flicking between the rest of the armies' colossal forces, too, which hadn't yet moved. 'How come that lot are just staying put?'

'Waiting for orders,' Liss supposed. 'Both sides want the hill. Their strategies for what happens next will depend on who gets it. And while the Doctor's magicks—'

'Sonicky science stuff.'

'—yes, that, while that's in place, the armies can't get at each other.'

That was, of course, Fate's cue to fizzle out whatever impossible barrier had sprung up between the two opposing forces. The Doctor shouted encouragement to her horse to gallop faster still. Behind her, Ryan saw a massive hulk of horn and wolf-hide tear away from the Roman scrum of horses and people, its claws tearing great chunks from the ground as it ran straight for the Huns, its howl like a clarion calling across the battlefield.

'Strava,' said Liss. 'War beasts given to the Visigoths by the Tenctrama.'

'And, whaddyaknow, they gave them to the Huns too,' Ryan said with a shudder. The beasts on each side looked the same; Ryan wondered how the generals would tell them apart when they fought each other. But it seemed the issue wouldn't arise – the Strava ignored each other completely, and only tore into the cavalry. War cries, and the screams of men and horses, rose up from the battleground, as the whistle and thud of flying arrows looped into a sickening beat. The Strava were soon stuck so full of swords and spears they looked more like hairy porcupines, but they didn't seem to feel it. They pounded through the ranks, taking down all within reach.

Ryan turned his eyes from the carnage back to the Doctor and Yaz as they rode up and jumped down from the horse. The Doctor reached him first and grabbed him so close, and gratefully he buried his face in her shoulder, breathed in her scent of camomile and engine oil. Yaz piled in and made it into a group hug.

'So good to see you!' the Doctor said. 'Are you all right?'

'Just about,' said Ryan.

'Where's Graham?' she went on.

'I saw Graham!' Yaz revealed. 'When I was in the Tenctrama ship, they could see him in the Roman camp. They know about the healing gel.'

The Doctor and Ryan looked at her and both said, 'Huh?'

Yaz nodded. 'Graham killed one of them in a bath with it!'

'What the …?' Ryan was thoroughly confused. 'Graham had a bath with one of those witch things?'

Yaz grimaced. 'No, I think she fell in the water.'

'Explains why Inkri told me we were messing up her harvest,' the Doctor said. 'The gel generates living cells to counter genetic damage, which must make it poison to the Tenctrama. But where's Graham now?'

'He is with Vitus,' said Liss, 'and safer than we are here.'

Yaz pointed to the Roman girl and mouthed at Ryan, 'Who's she?'

'Better option than the Strava.' Ryan pointed behind them at one of the bloodied beasts, which had torn free from the battle and was limping towards them across the battlefield.

'We must go.' Liss strode back towards the opening in the ground. 'This is no place for a reunion.'

'Wait,' said the Doctor, facing down the Strava. Gold sparkled in the dark slits of its eyes as it grew closer, rock-sized teeth bared, a growl building in its belly. 'I want to know where these things came from.'

Ryan grabbed her arm. 'I'm pretty sure I know where we'll end up if it gets us!'

But the Doctor had pulled out the sonic screwdriver. Ryan heard the same deep, penetrating vibration he'd heard back in the forest before the crows had broken off their attack, and his legs almost gave way beneath him. The Strava lowered its tusked head as if about to charge, but then it twitched and huffed out a long, steaming breath.

'It's stopping,' Yaz realised, clutching her ears.

'The sonic's interfering with the command centre of his brain,' the Doctor said, checking the readings. 'The Strava aren't living creatures in the conventional sense – they've been created and animated by the Tenctrama, and conditioned to attack certain targets.' She scowled. 'But how do they do it? How do the Tenctrama appropriate life like that?'

'Or death like that,' Liss said, teeth gritted as the vibration shook on.

The Strava raised its head and roared, snapping its jaws.

The Doctor made the sonic buzz more loudly. 'I can't stop it,' she shouted. 'Get behind me! The will to kill is too strong.'

'We have to go!' Liss shouted.

'What about Bittenmane?' Yaz pressed her hand to the horse's neck. His sides were flecked with foam, and he was shaking his head and snorting in distress. 'He can't come with us down there.'

The Doctor pressed the sonic into Ryan's hand. 'Take over.'

'Me?' Ryan's heart flipped.

'Of course, you. You've got this.' The Doctor put her head against Bittenmane's. 'You saved our lives, you clever horse. Thank you. Now you have to go.' She slapped the horse on his rump, whistled, and with a bob of his head he turned and galloped away. 'That's it, run!'

Liss was staring. 'That horse really seemed to understand!'

The Doctor smiled. 'Well, I happen to be fluent in several equine dialects …'

'How about we all get giddying up, yeah?' Sonic clamped in a death grip, staring down the slavering Strava, Ryan backed away, waving the Doctor, Liss and Yaz back towards the tunnel with his spare hand. 'Shift!'

Chapter 25

From his vantage point on the left flank, Aetius watched as chaos engulfed the hillside. Bad enough that Attila's new witch had clearly granted him magicks with which to shield his forces, but to see the Strava running wild and unrestrained …

Naelsa had provided ten of the supernatural beasts to the Visigoths, claiming they would break the ranks of the Hun army, allowing the Roman cavalry to simply pick off the fleeing warriors. Except, of course, the Huns proved to have their own Strava, and just as many. Now they were destroying his forces, just as his were tearing through theirs.

Aetius had never feared battle, but this … This was not war, it was simply carnage. The Strava refused to attack each other, and since they were already dead, they were near impossible to bring down. It took forty or fifty men to destroy a single Strava, with most dying in the attempt.

With dread prickling along his spine, Aetius saw those dead men rise again from the crimson mud of the plains and jerk back into combat: the dead falling on the living, the beasts rampaging on, ignoring the dead.

The metal plate tucked behind his breastplate buzzed and shone with familiar energy. Aetius swore – he hated such unnatural devices! – but turned and discreetly placed the talk-box to his ear. 'Well?'

'Licinia, sir. We have captured Attila's witch and removed her from the field via the catacomb vent, Eastern Sector. She can give the Huns no further magicks.'

Aetius's tired features almost found a smile. 'Very well,' he said, 'watch her closely.' Then he put the talk-box back behind his breastplate and signalled to his First Centurion. 'Prepare the catapults and the spear shooters,' he said. 'We must bring down the Huns' beasts with more efficiency—'

'Here, Flavius Aetius!' Theodoric, king of the Visigoths, approached with his bodyguard and Mekimma, the last of the hags, in tow.

Aetius stared at Mekimma. 'Why did you bring this witch?'

'She refuses to control her monsters. I no longer protect her.'

The crone looked placid, unperturbed. 'You wished for beasts that could eat an army. You have those beasts.'

'So too do the Huns!' Theodoric's face, or that part of it that wasn't beard, had flushed bright red. 'My faith in you is spent, witch. Flavius Aetius, you have spoken against the Tenctrama many times, and your sciences saved me when hers could not. I bring Mekimma to you now to punish as you will.'

You mean, thought Aetius, *that you fear the old woman and want me to incur the Tenctrama's wrath in your place.* The crone was nodding as if eavesdropping on his thoughts, the lopsided smile more of a sneer now. He was aware the men were watching him, waiting for decisive leadership, and knew too that the Tenctrama stood condemned by her actions.

He had no choice.

Aetius took a deep breath. 'Witch, I believe that either your magicks are spent, or else you act in treason to our cause. You cannot heal the sick. You cannot call off your war-beasts. You cannot prevent the dead from rising. I, Flavius Aetius, Protector of Rome and all her allies, swear now that you will die if you will not perform as we demand.'

'Very well.' Mekimma's smile grew wider. 'Grant me, then, one last request.' She turned to stare up at Theodoric. 'This man has been corrupted by healing magicks. The wheat is made chaff. He must be removed.'

Theodoric glowered, but Aetius saw the tremble in his hand as he raised it against her. 'You would threaten a king, crone?'

Mekimma darted out her withered fingers, dug them in Theodoric's face. 'I kill kings like summer flies.'

'Stop her!' Aetius snapped to his guards, but no one moved, staring in horror. Theodoric was already glowing red as hellfire. A stink of roasting flesh and burning hair engulfed the reeling onlookers, as the Visigoth king exploded into embers and his bodyguards fell to their knees, moaning with fear.

Outraged, sickened, Aetius spoke with his sword: with both hands, he drove it down into the witch's back. The point of the sword embedded in the mud, sticking her there.

Aetius had seen many things that he could not explain, many that he had tried to conceal, suppress and file away. None touched a deeper terror inside him than the sight of Mekimma's head twisting slowly through a hundred and eighty degrees to stare up at him. 'This is not your war, human,' she rasped, a golden-bright light building inside her. 'It is our reaping.'

The next moment she exploded in light, a million fiery trails blistering across the battlespace.

Aetius rounded on his troops, many of whom were backing away in terror. 'No one deserts,' he growled, 'or I'll watch you rise from the dead here and now. Fetch the spear shooters, and the catapults. Aim for the Strava and scatter the Huns.' He turned to Theodoric's guards. 'Tell your commanders and your soldiers that your king died bravely in battle ... that his last words were that they must fight under his son, Thorismund, who is the new king.' The guards nodded, turned and ran. 'And tell them to stay alive, damn it!'

'The Huns, sir!' a messenger called.

Aetius already knew what news the boy brought; he could feel the rumble through his feet, the pounding of a million hooves. He looked across the battlespace and saw Attila committing the full force of his cavalry into the field. His own commanders were already responding, the infantry holding up their shields as the skies darkened with the first rain of arrows.

Aetius pulled his sword from the ground and wiped the blade on the mud, as his trebuchets sent boulders as big as men flying towards the hillside. He crossed to where his horse was being dressed in the last of its armour by a stable lad. He remembered himself as a child, doing the same for his general on another battlefield in another distant land, such a long time ago.

Once again it was time to fight.

Chapter 26

Consus had never felt so scared. Freedom should mean he could do anything at all. In practice, it saw him frozen with indecision on the higher ground east of the plain, watching the battle unfold.

Such a spectacle he'd never seen. Exotic beasts tearing through the far flank of the battlefield as spears and boulders carved their way through the sky! It was like some terrible tale from the Greek myths, made true. And across the plains, Consus saw that the Huns' reputation as the fiercest fighters in the world was no story. There had to be a thousand riders in each regiment, galloping in huge circles before breaking away in formation to confront the enemy. Hundreds of Huns, advancing in waves on the fastest horses, each man loosing seven or eight arrows at the same cluster of Roman infantry, seeking to break the defensive line, then peeling away to collect fresh arrows from the ammunition holders at the rear, while the next wave came forward to do the same. Even as the Huns' war horses galloped pell-mell over the churned-up ground, their riders would shoot from all angles – leaning back until they were horizontal to shoot arrows far behind them, or twisting forward to shoot lying on their fronts. There was almost a poetry to it! Consus had always loved poetry, loved especially those nights when Aetius, lying on his couch and weary with the world and his problems, would make him read aloud from Ennius or Naevius.

For the hundredth time Consus fought the urge to return to the camp, to throw himself on the mercy of his master. But Aetius was a man of dark secrets; for all he claimed to detest magicks, he knew wizardry. Consus had heard him talk to the air and receive answers. And when he'd sliced Consus open like a joint of meat to be healed by the Briton's unnatural powers, he'd gone too far. Aetius had brought witches rising and horrible, unnatural death into the heart of his army home. Consus wanted none of it.

And from the way the battle was going … the impossible terror on the field, the dead jumping up from the ground to overcome the living … would there even be a camp to return to? Consus glanced again at the scar on his arm, the puckered line that looked years old already, and cringed. He felt marked by magick. Perhaps he could hide himself among the people of Orléans, help the town elders rebuild in the wake of the barbarian siege. He was bright, he could read Latin and Greek, he could find someone to take him under his wing. He should leave now, begin the journey today, put miles between him and these hairy barbarians. Against the odds, he had survived. Consus was a slave no longer. He was free.

As he turned, decisive at last, Consus saw the witch-woman hovering behind him, her clawed hands outstretched. He opened his mouth to scream, but her dirt-caked talons were already pressing into his temples and heat was coursing through his body. The witch's narrowed eyes blazed like molten gold.

'You are poisoned,' she said, in what sounded like two voices, her own and something deeper. 'The harvest must be pure.'

Then Consus saw nothing but the flames that consumed him.

From over Vitus's shoulder, Graham watched Consus die and the Tenctrama leave the blaze like a wizened old phoenix, nursing his palpitations in the undergrowth. He'd hoped the woods would be safer now with the dead men all migrating to the battlefield, hoped that they might just make the journey back to Legion of Smoke HQ without something horrible happening.

Stupid, Graham told himself. *Why would you ever think that?*

'The witches have begun to murder for its own sake?' Even Vitus seemed shaken by what they'd seen. 'Is there not enough death for them this day?'

'Consus wasn't poisoned,' Graham said quietly. 'I healed him.'

'May his soul rest well,' said Vitus, 'wherever he has gone.'

Graham nodded, troubled, as Vitus dug his heels into their horse and they broke through the bracken, galloping away, stirring flecks of ash as they departed.

*

Inkri nodded with satisfaction as Mekimma and Enkalo returned to the lair.

'The Visigoth king is removed,' said Mekimma.

'And the slave of Aetius,' Enkalo said. 'Now, Attila must be removed.'

'Not yet. His army will lose its spirit and flee without him. Let him fight on to the last as the bodies build around him ... then let the last Huns fall in despair as they watch their king burn.' Inkri closed her eyes, wheezed a long breath inwards as if inhaling the horror far below. 'We are so close to the trigger point ... so close.'

'The location of the Doctor and her friends is less clear,' Enkalo said. 'They do not carry our corruption. They are harder to trace.'

'They will be found,' Inkri said. 'They will burn.'

Now the Doctor and Yaz were back, Ryan didn't want to let either of them out of his sight. They'd swapped the barest details of their adventures and experiences, but now the Doctor was off striding ahead as always, like she was trying to outrun her own coattails. She stopped abruptly, attention taken by something on the glowing wall – knowing her, probably a ladybird or something. Ryan took the moment to check on Yaz. She looked tired and strained, shivering in the dank atmosphere of the catacombs. Ryan pulled off his hoodie and tried to put it round her shoulders.

Yaz shook her head, shrugged it off. 'I don't need it.' Then she sighed, turned to face him. 'Sorry, Ryan. This has been a tough day.'

'For me too.' He forced a cheeky smile. 'I had to walk through a ton of tunnels and make awkward conversation with this Roman girl.'

'He's beautiful, isn't he?' Liss said behind him, making him jump. 'And so caring.'

'Wow!' Yaz raised her eyebrows. 'Clearly you two have been getting along very well.'

Ryan felt bashful. 'Yeah. It's all good.'

Liss pointed to the Doctor. 'And you both get to travel with *her*.'

'It's me who gets to travel with them!' The Doctor's smile faltered as she grew pensive. 'I wonder if I should pop back out and find Attila. Try to make him stop the fighting.'

'Huh?' Ryan was glad of the change of subject but not its implications. 'What are you on about?'

'We need to stop the killing.'

'He's Attila the Hun, he'll kill you!' Yaz protested.

'What about Aetius?' Ryan looked at Licinia. 'Liss, you called your boss and told him about the Doctor – can't you make him see reason and stop fighting?'

'I can't imagine he'll listen. Perhaps if Vitus tells him too?' She produced her talk-box. 'Vitus? If you can, lend me your ear …'

'Ha!' At this, the Doctor swung round, delighted. 'I swear the TARDIS telepathic circuits have a sense of humour. Wait, you shouldn't have anachronistic technology like that, Liss! Just like you shouldn't have dioxylithium glow-algae from the Cygnus cluster on the walls, here. Naughty Roman lady. I think you're probably nice, though, aren't you?'

Liss beamed. 'Probably.'

'I knew it.' The Doctor swiped the talk-box and peered at it. 'Well! This looks like a Velucron comms-link.'

'Velucron?' Licinia gazed at her in still more awe. 'You can name the relics?'

'Yes, and with really big words! It's a gift of mine. I'm the Doctor, by the way.'

'Of course you are. That's why we came for you.' She frowned suddenly. 'You know, you really look nothing like your votive effigy.'

'My what?'

Suddenly the metal glowed blue. 'Licinia,' Vitus's voice came from inside, 'are you all right?'

The Doctor adopted a cut-glass posh accent. 'Liss can't come to the phone right now, who's this?'

'Doc?' Graham's voice came over loud and clear, and there was instant pandemonium as Ryan and Yaz burst forward to grab the Doctor's wrist and lean in to speak to him.

'Graham!' Yaz cried.

'You're all right?' said Ryan.

'How did he know it was me?' the Doctor marvelled.

'I'm a whole lot better for hearing you lot!' Graham told them. 'Doc, Yaz, we saw you on the battlefield, and Ryan, when I lost you—'

'If I might be allowed to continue?' Vitus must've snatched back the comms-link. 'Liss, I take it you've found my target.'

'He was gonna kill you, boss!' Graham shouted.

'He had *orders* to kill you.' Deftly Liss swiped the metal plate from the Doctor's grip. 'He was never going to act on them, though.'

'I was there, I can vouch,' said Ryan.

'Vitus,' Liss went on, 'I'm in the catacombs with Ryan and his friends. The Doctor says we need to—'

'How is our great enigma?' Vitus asked eagerly. 'Is it the man or the woman?'

'The woman!'

'And what's she like?'

'Impatient!' The Doctor snatched the comms-link. 'Vitus, hi. You must get hold of Aetius and tell him to stop the fighting. Liss will do the same.'

'Stop fighting? But Aetius will never surrender to the Huns.'

'That's what the Tenctrama are banking on, but we need the battle to stop. The more dead there are, the better things go for the witches.' The Doctor closed her eyes and squeezed the comms-link tightly. 'Now, get on to him, persuade him, one of you, both of you, please!'

'All right.' Vitus paused. 'Liss, we're making our way back to base. Careful if you go outside – there are Tenctrama active out here. We saw one appear from nowhere and burn up a deserter at random.'

'Burn up? That's new.'

'She said he was poisoned,' Graham put in, 'but he was tip-top, I'd used the healing gel on him earlier. S'pose it might've been revenge for the one that died in Aetius's tent ...'

Yaz took hold of the comms-link. 'She *was* poisoned. Healing gel in the water. I dunno how it works but her energy was all messed up. They had to vent her energy from the Pit.'

You could almost hear Graham's frown. 'Come again?'

'No, she couldn't,' said the Doctor, thoughtfully. 'That was it for her.'

'Get here as soon as you can, Graham, yeah?' Yaz held the comms-link up for Ryan.

'Bye,' he said. 'And take care, all right?'

'Half-left,' said Graham.

Yaz rolled her eyes in perfect tandem with Ryan.

Liss stepped between them and took the comms-link. 'I'd best try and call the old man.'

'Yes. Do.' The Doctor pushed her hair off her forehead, deep in thought. 'Vented from the Pit, energy lost, not to be recycled … Perhaps because the gel brings life and the Tenctrama feed on death and decay.' She gestured around. 'That's probably why they took over these catacombs, way, way back and turned them into a secret hidey-hole.'

Liss stared at her, gobsmacked. 'What?'

Yaz shook her head. 'Doctor, their base is in the sky, not underground.'

'Sure, *now* it is. But ten, eleven hundred years ago, no. A grub stays in the mud till it's grown. Only then does it poke its head out and fly up to the tree.' She mimed a wriggling thing with her finger. 'See, newborn, or freshly projected from inside this Pit of theirs, they'd need a place to hide underground and grow stronger. Right here, down among the dead, with access to a quiet little town of the living nearby. Growing. Learning. Gathering samples and intelligence. Adapting their DNA to fit in with the locals, beginning the cycle.'

'Where's your evidence?' Liss demanded.

'Hidden.' The Doctor grinned suddenly. 'Luckily I have a nose for sniffing out alien tech. Honestly, I do!' She tapped the wall, and now Ryan saw what she'd really been looking at there – a small slate barely visible in the algae-light. 'Alien Tech 101: this is a door handle.'

She buzzed the sonic over it, and a section of solid rock rumbled open. Cold, stinking air wafted out from the hidden cave. Ryan cringed not just from the smell but from the scene revealed: there was an altar – or more like, a stone operating table surrounded by strange instruments – with a twisted human skeleton lying across it.

'Who was that?' Ryan wondered aloud.

'A subject in a Tenctrama experiment,' the Doctor supposed, nosing about. 'There'll have been so many over the years. Inkri and her kind checking that their genetic tampering was progressing correctly as it was passed on through the generations … Making corrections and adjustments.'

Liss looked at her. 'What do you mean?'

The Doctor came out of the cave and explained all she'd learned from Inkri in Attila's camp. Yaz watched as Liss grew greener in the pale light of the tunnel.

'You were right, then, Ryan, about the grain the Tenctrama gave us.' Liss was clutching her stomach. 'And the Antonine plague they predicted – they started that, didn't they? Those that survived were … changed somehow?'

'Who knows what antibodies or proteins were generated by that infection …' The Doctor looked Liss up and down and beamed. 'Smart observations. I like her, Ryan. Well found.'

'She kind of found me.'

'I chased him for miles,' Liss confided.

'He's so worth it, though, isn't he?' said the Doctor, slapping Ryan's shoulder fondly.

Ryan's smile faded as the tunnel shook with unknown things thundering overhead – horses? Strava? Thousands of soldiers running for their lives …?

'Maybe we could all chase Ryan,' Yaz said with panto enthusiasm, 'away from here.'

'Come on, then.' The Doctor had found another small slate further along the tunnel wall, and now scanned it with the sonic. 'Let's explore Tenctrama technology a little further …'

Chapter 27

Sweating and tense as a bowstring at full stretch, Attila watched as his men swarmed over an injured Strava, trying to bring it down without falling prey to tusks or teeth. The beast looked to have bathed in blood, shrieking blind defiance as the blows rained down. Its victims stirred at its clawed feet, revived as glistening flesh bubbled up from inside to seal gaping wounds.

The scene had grown far too familiar.

Attila turned, took a flask from his bodyguards and drank deeply. Battle thus far had been joined in two successive waves, colossal and confused. The jerking corpses had seized the chance to rejoin the battle, until the once-parched mud of the plains now oozed blood with every footfall. The worst of it was that after all the horror and carnage, it was Roman forces that held the hill.

The Strava was finally dispatched, and a ragged cheer rose from the survivors of the work. Attila knew he must capitalise on any victory, however small. 'You see how we triumph over the beasts of Rome!' he roared at his men like the lion they knew him to be. 'You see how panic drives the enemy to the high ground. They fear our might on the open plain. The glory of this battle is promised to us!'

And yet even as he harangued his dogs, he felt uneasy. The pale, gory dead still stood close in the ranks, murmuring and twitching. He'd always told his followers that victory was won through sheer force – hack through the nerves of the enemy and they cannot lift limbs against you. And yet here were warriors on both sides who could stand with the bones broken from their bodies. These dead Huns followed no order to retreat or repose, only to attack.

But he knew in his heart: *It is not me these dead men follow, and not me they fight for. They are simply the puppets of witches.* Like the Strava, that had no master but bloodlust, these creatures of dead flesh wore the masks of Huns and Romans over the faces of devils.

He looked up to the sky, and in the gathering clouds he seemed to see the laughing faces of Inkri and her Tenctrama sisters. *If I am to die,* Attila thought, *let me be slain by men whose hearts beat with vengeance for all I have taken from their lands, not at the jerking sword of a brainless dolt.*

The mutter of distant thunder proved to be hoofbeats across the plain, as the banners of Rome took flight towards the Hun front lines. Well, let them come! Attila was ready to lead a new charge. He rose on his magnificent white horse and signalled with his sword for his army to follow him, once again.

Fifes and horns swanked and blared, and drums burst the eardrums as they rolled, but soon all music was eclipsed by the shouts rising from fifty thousand throats in one overwhelming roar, Attila's loudest of all: '*Hoooy-raaaaah!*'

As he followed the Doctor through the Tenctrama chambers hollowed from the rock, Ryan's nerves were jangling hard enough to be heard. Yaz stayed close beside him while Liss brought up the rear, still trying to contact her Roman boss on the battlefield. Never any luck.

The Doctor had led them through more 'operating rooms' like the first they'd found, each with the bones of a different victim abandoned on the altar. Beyond those, a wall had rumbled open onto a long, narrow chamber bored out of the rock. Huge misshapen crystals hung down from the ceiling, while the floor was covered with soil and the wispy husks of ancient plants.

'The Tenctrama's crops.' Liss surveyed the remains. 'Their gift to us.'

'Let's hope you *aren't* what you eat,' Ryan murmured.

She raised an eyebrow. 'Because I'd be dead?'

'I didn't mean that!' Ryan protested.

'Smooth,' Yaz told him. 'Doctor, what're you hoping to find here?'

'Connections,' she said vaguely, activating the next slate in the wall.

A new door opened, releasing a zoo-cage stink so thick it nearly choked Ryan. 'Ugh, that's well rank!'

'What happened here?' Yaz pointed to the distorted, desiccated bodies of huge beasts littering the floor of this latest laboratory. 'What. The. Hell?'

Liss was clutching her stomach. 'They look a bit like Strava.'

'Steps along the way.' The Doctor had stooped to inspect the bodies. 'Putting evil into evolution. But how do they do it?'

'Do what?' said Yaz.

'How do they twist death back into life in a form that they can control?'

Ryan reached out to touch a cracked and blackened outgrowth of crystal, projecting from the wall. A chunk of it fell away with a noisy crash that made everyone jump. 'Sorry,' he said quickly.

'There's something inside.' Yaz pulled out a tube that looked to be made of some metallic stone. 'They used stuff like this in their lair, for controlling things.'

'Maybe the crystal was a holder,' Ryan suggested. 'Like the holster thing Nan had for her remote.'

'Or a charger.' The Doctor took hold of the weird device, turning it over in her hands.

'I don't understand your words,' said Liss. 'You're saying this is a Tenctrama tool?'

'Yes, it is.' The Doctor worked the sonic, and the tube glittered with golden light. 'From the way Inkri was talking, I knew they had to have used something like this.' Three holographic crystals grew from one end like blown bubbles, helical structures turning inside. 'A genetic manipulator …'

Yaz worked out what the patterns looked like ahead of Ryan. 'Is that DNA?'

The Doctor bestowed a brief but brilliant smile on her. 'It is.'

'What's DNA?' asked Liss.

'Do Not Ask,' said the Doctor. 'But since I like you: basically, you can't see it or touch it, but all life's made up of it, one way or another.'

'No, life is made up of the humours,' Liss stated. 'Blood, phlegm, black bile and yellow bile …'

'Or you could call them adenine, thymine, cytosine and guanine. Same difference. Kind of.' The Doctor tapped the manipulator. 'In here we have the "humours" from several animals – lion, rhino, wolf, others – combined and augmented to create a hybrid creature. A Strava.'

'The Tenctrama must've travelled all over the world,' said Ryan, 'finding the animals that made the deadliest killer.'

Liss nodded. 'Some of the old depictions do show them with wild animals.'

'But what's the final ingredient?' The Doctor was pulling at the glowing crystals, drawing out new ones, shifting them about like a juggler working on her act. 'What kicks in at the moment of death to rewire brain and body in a new paradigm …?' She plucked a different pattern from another crystal, a distorted shadow of the other DNA designs. 'Oh, I see, *you* do. You kick in.'

Yaz shrugged. 'Tenctrama DNA?'

'A kind of genetic energy. Essence of Tenctrama.' The Doctor winked at Liss. 'A *fifth* humour.' She rushed back to the dead plants in the chamber beyond, touched the other end of the tube to a withered leaf. A black spark jumped between the two, and the Doctor buzzed the sonic again, switching through the glowing bubbles with their spinning patterns. 'There'll be a match,' she muttered, 'there'll be a match ... there!'

The same dark, distorted DNA pattern spun slowly in the golden light.

'It's there in the crop?' Ryan blew out a wondering whistle. 'And I bet it's in the dead men walking too, right?'

'Has to be,' the Doctor said. 'The Tenctrama appropriate life – properly treated life, at least – and their essence binds with it somehow, destroys it and reanimates it with the Tenctrama will.'

'Reprograms it,' Yaz suggested. 'So, we get dead birds that spy or attack on command, dead soldiers only fixated on killing their old enemies ...'

'And dead Strava who'll go for humans but leave each other alone,' said Ryan.

'At least for as long as it suits the Tenctrama.' The Doctor turned to Liss. 'Relics! That's what you said, when we came into the catacombs, that I could name the relics. Plural. So, it's not just comms-links – what other weird stuff have you got?'

'It's kept in the Hidden Hall,' Liss said.

'That's miles away,' Ryan sighed.

'I might know a short cut. Connections, remember? The Tenctrama are all about fluidity.' The Doctor studied the special slate she'd called a door handle. 'You know how they come and go on the air? It's not magicks at work. I've already isolated the transport bandwidth ...'

'Didn't get us far outside,' Yaz reminded her. 'You said we were locked out.'

'Of the network between Earth and sky, yes. But now we're under the earth—'

'Different network,' said Ryan.

'And with luck and a fair wind …!' The Doctor sonicked, and a layout plan, presumably of the catacombs, was picked out in trails of golden light. 'Here are the spaces the Tenctrama colonised.' The Doctor tapped the sonic against a large square to the left of the plan. 'Hidden Hall?'

'Looks like it!' Liss clapped.

'Come on, then.' The Doctor walked into the wall almost absent-mindedly.

With a hum of power, she glowed and disappeared.

'She opened a tunnel in the air!' Liss pulled Ryan after her as she ran towards the wall. 'Oh, my poor feet are so happy!'

Yaz watched them shine gold and vanish, leaving her alone. She felt suddenly sad and afraid, and thought of Bittenmane, alone on the plains outside. 'Stay safe, boy,' she said quietly.

'I am safe, girl!' said Ryan, glowing gold as he stuck out of the wall. 'Bless.'

Yaz frowned. 'I was actually talking to Attila's horse!'

'Bittenmane. Right. Course you were.'

'I was!'

'Look, I'm here chasing you, Yaz, cos you're so worth it.'

'Oh, shut up …'

Still grumbling, Yaz followed him through the invisible door in the wall.

Attila leaned forward in the saddle, gripping his new mount hard with his knees. His banner, silver-white, billowed in the wind overhead. Flanking him, left and right, in glittering armour, his bodyguards rode with huge leather shields, their only duty to watch their master and keep all spears and blows from reaching him. Two more men rode close behind him leading saddled horses beside their own, so that if his own mount was struck by axe or arrow he could switch to another. The pounding of hooves, the red dust clouds kicked up, the snorting of the frightened horses: Attila blanked them all out, focused only on the dense ranks of the enemy ahead, on Roman heads peeping over shields.

His horse was flying like the wind, and its breast struck into the front line with a grinding crunch. Bellowing his war cry, he brought his wooden mace down on Roman infantrymen, swinging wildly, his bodyguards deflecting blows and dealing out their own. A spear thrust up clean through the neck of his horse and jabbed against Attila's stomach; in an instant he brought down his arm to snap the spear shaft, gripped the top section and hurled it down into the screaming mass of men. Convulsing, his horse trampled its attacker, but Attila rolled off nimbly and jumped into the saddle of the free horse to his right, pricking its sides with his heels. Behind him, he saw Chokona leading the next wave of attack on a fine grey stallion, letting fly his quiver of arrows; Attila led his men away from the infantry line so that Chokona's unit could take their place and continue the onslaught. So it would go on, wave upon wave of horsemen crashing into the ranks until the infantry was broken.

As he left the front line of battle, Attila threw a look back over his shoulder: already the Romans slain were returning to their feet. They climbed over piles of fallen horses and threw themselves without fear into the paths of the Hun cavalry, ignoring the blows from sword and mace. Chokona's shriek somehow rose above the mêlée, and before the sight was snatched away by fresh carnage, Attila saw the point of a spear push through his chieftain's back.

A spear in the hands of a Hun.

That was when Attila realised that many of the dead rising back to attack his forces were Huns themselves. Stunned, he turned his horse in a tight circle and brought it to a standstill, unwilling to trust his senses. But it was true: brother now killed brother in a bloody free-for-all, ignoring all orders, all pleas, all screams. The Romans and their allies were clashing too, stabbing and spearing anyone who came close, no matter their allegiance.

Attila became aware that his bodyguards were staring at him, waiting for his orders. He turned away, raised his sword and stabbed twice at the air. The bugler was watching and sounded a long, falling note, the signal to retreat.

He rode away from the howling, the blood, the madness, his silver flag trailing like a ghost above the galloping cavalry. Attila knew now: this was no longer a fight for Gaul and the future of Rome's empire.

The battle now was between the living and the dead.

Chapter 28

Imagining the terror and confusion down below, Inkri turned to Enkalo and laughed. 'Our corpse warriors are now compelled to kill any in reach. The deaths, indiscriminate, will come faster.'

'All the waiting. The long, long centuries.' Enkalo caressed her sister's face. 'We will be beautiful again.'

'But the Doctor has not yet been found.' Inkri narrowed her eyes. 'The search must be extended. She and her accomplices must be destroyed.'

'That's another poor fella those witches have offed.' Graham stared sadly at the pile of ash in the merchant's wagon; they'd paused there on their way to the secret cemetery where the gang was waiting.

'Why burn up his body?' Vitus wondered. 'They did the same with the slave.'

'They must really hate that healing gel,' said Graham. 'I used it on his face, his nose had been bashed in.'

Vitus looked at him. 'Using alien technology on ordinary citizens is irresponsible.'

'Oi! Who blasted those Huns to bits with his ray gun?' Graham sighed, thinking now of Theodoric, and if this fate might have befallen him too. 'Excuse me trying to help people. How was I to know I was marking them out for … this.'

'Well, there's nothing we can do for any of them now,' Vitus said. 'And we'd better get you to cover. If the Tenctrama are killing anyone who's touched that stuff …'

Graham gulped. 'I could be next!'

Ryan sat in the Hidden Hall with Yaz, watching as the Doctor managed to make even more of a mess of Liss's files. Just now Liss was trying for the twentieth time to contact Aetius on the comms-link, hiding her eyes as yet another trunk full of electronic bric-a-brac was upended over the old stone floor.

'Be careful, Doctor!' Liss pleaded. 'Some of those artefacts are hundreds of years old.'

'And then some,' the Doctor agreed.

'If you could tell me what you're looking for …?'

'Anything useful,' she declared. 'I'm hoping I'll know it when I find it.'

A grey, egg-shaped device rolled across the room. Ryan stooped to pick it up but knocked over a blue steel cylinder as he did so. 'Oops. Sorry, Liss.'

'Mind that Arcturan grenade, by the way,' the Doctor went on. 'Might still be live.'

Yaz frowned. 'The what might be what?'

Freezing, Ryan swallowed hard. 'Which one is the grenade?'

'Both. Blue bit goes into grey, makes a boom.' The Doctor looked up, frowning. 'How did I miss you lot getting invaded by Arcturans? Well, maybe it was just a scout. I can't be here every time an alien scout-ship crash-lands on Earth. I expect the Tenctrama got rid of it. They'd want to protect their investment in Earth's animal life.'

Liss put down the stubbornly silent comms-link. 'How did they come to Earth, anyway?'

'I imagine this Pit of theirs can project them over vast tracts of space to planets with life forms they can exploit.' The Doctor was prowling like a caged cat, looking on shelves and in dusty corners for something that she clearly felt ought to be there. 'Then they bed down below ground, working to replenish the Pit so the whole thing can start over again.'

'An invisible Pit that hangs in the sky for a thousand years?'

'More likely a part of their spaceship. Puts itself into geostationary orbit high above the lair, hides itself in a teleportation loop and waits in hibernation.'

'Teleportation loop?' Yaz tried to get her head round it. 'D'you mean their ship hides out in the gap between leaving one place and arriving at another?'

'Spot on!' The Doctor smiled at her fondly. 'I think the Tenctrama operate as energy projections in a fluid state of flux. Their physical form is a manifestation of the animating energy.'

Liss and Ryan looked at each other blankly.

'Death liberates that energy, renews it,' the Doctor went on. 'If you "kill" the body, the energy unravels to be conducted back up to the Tenctrama lair. And as Yaz knows, it can take the living along for the ride.'

'I'm just glad you got out OK,' Ryan said. 'What was it like up there, Yaz?'

'A cross between a dead forest and a cathedral.' She shuddered. 'Stone altars, like the one we saw in that room. Dead trees that grew sort of scanner crystals like fruits ...'

'Think I'll pass on one of those for my five a day,' Ryan said.

'Ryan, that's it!' The Doctor looked up suddenly and stared into space. 'What do you call the stone inside a peach or a plum or an apricot? A pit! A *Pit*! And inside the Pit ...'

'Is the seed,' Yaz realised. 'All the potential for new life.'

'Or new *death*. For our poor, mutated Tenctrama, it's spaceship and racebank and nourisher all in one.' The Doctor went back to searching through a crate. 'Well done, you lot. You're brilliant. You cracked it.'

Liss gave up on her comms-link for now and sighed, clearly dubious. 'Seems a strange sort of life cycle for anything.'

'Cicadas!' the Doctor retorted. 'There's one species that spends seventeen years maturing underground, then, boom! Two months above ground as adults, just time to mate and lay eggs, and then they die.'

Liss looked at Ryan. 'Well, that is strange too.'

'Must make it hard for predators to find you,' Ryan said. 'Maybe that's what the Tenctrama go in for.'

'And why the Doctor being here has freaked them out,' Yaz added.

'Guess it's like what you told us about that high-flying vulture back in the TARDIS. You know, creatures adapting weirdly to their environments.'

'But sometimes they need a little help. Especially when their own genetic make-up has been so corrupted by the weapons used in their wars. Aha! *Voila!*' She scooped up a handful of small metallic tubes from the bottom of a casket. 'Translation units.'

'For translating what?,' said Ryan. 'Languages?'

'The language of DNA, transcribed in Tenctrama ink.' The Doctor produced the manipulator from her pocket, and slotted one of the tubes inside. 'They didn't only use this stuff to create Strava and GM crops. By bonding with human DNA they could approximate your form, walk among you, put their plans in motion.'

'Why are there so many of those … "units"?' asked Liss.

'The wars that destroyed the Tenctrama's old civilisation made that "fifth humour" we talked about incredibly destructive. It must have taken a lot of tries to stabilise Tenctrama essence in living matter.' She nodded to the mummified husk in the corner. 'Spawned so many mutations.'

Ryan could hardly take it all in. 'The stuff they've had to do to survive …'

'Survival's all that matters. Nature's prerogative, even when it's against all nature.' The Doctor sighed. 'You know, there's a parasite that lives in certain ants, and it mutates their abdomens to resemble red berries. Birds like berries, so they're tricked into eating the ants. Then they spread the parasite through their droppings. More ants gather the droppings to feed to their young, and they unwittingly pass on the infection.'

Liss looked sick. 'You're saying that human beings are the berry-ants?'

'Oh, no. Not them alone.' The Doctor looked grave. 'I'm afraid that Inkri and her friends have made nice bright berries out of your entire animal kingdom.'

'Question is,' said Ryan, 'how are we going to stop them?'

A two-edged voice sounded from the darkness behind them. 'You cannot.'

Ryan spun round. A Tenctrama was levitating through the air towards the Doctor, hair and sackcloth rags trailing behind her, talons outstretched.

Chapter 29

Ryan tried to run forward, to pull the Doctor away, but he found he could barely move; Yaz was the same, while Liss was completely frozen, perhaps because she'd lived her whole life with the Tenctrama's influence in the background.

The Doctor tried to run to one corner of the Hall but the crone overtook her in a heartbeat, fingers hooking towards her throat.

Then there was a sharp, spiteful zap of sound and a red light struck the Tenctrama. With a shriek of rage she exploded into glittering light.

Graham and Vitus were standing in the doorway. Graham was in Roman clothes, holding a ray gun. He looked as shocked as anyone that the Tenctrama had been blasted away. 'I . . . I didn't mean to kill her.'

'You didn't, Graham!' The Doctor ran to him. 'You only sent her packing. Good timing. Nice outfit!'

'The gang's back together!' Ryan said, his grin as wide as Yaz's.

'And you must be Vitus,' the Doctor went on, gripping his hand. 'Like the dance! Or you would be if you were a saint, anyway. Are you a saint?'

'Trust me, he's not,' Liss put in. 'How did that Tenctrama find us? Was it my horse roped up outside – did Reduxa give us away?'

'Inkri and her sisters must be monitoring events above ground,' the Doctor said. 'Perhaps they've been tracking Graham.'

Graham looked crestfallen. 'You think I led them straight to you?'

'They'd have found me in the end whatever you did. Anyway! Thanks for not assassinating me, Vitus, I appreciate it.'

Vitus stared. 'You look nothing like your votive offering.'

'So I gather. Did you get through to Aetius?'

'He actually got through to me,' Vitus said, 'I think. My talk-box glowed, but I could hear nothing but the sounds of war.'

'Probably butt-phoned you,' Ryan said.

'He what?'

'Called you by mistake,' Yaz said, replacing the Doctor's hand with her own. 'Hi there,' she said to Vitus with the briefest of glances at Ryan. 'My friends call me Yaz.'

Liss ran up to Vitus and embraced him, nudging Yaz aside. 'About time you got here, cousin!' She kissed Graham on the cheek. 'And that, my friend, was a mighty entrance.'

'Guess they weren't expecting ray guns from Romans.' Graham looked chuffed. 'Or Roman impersonators.'

'I don't think they'll be caught off guard again,' said the Doctor. 'And now they know where we are, and all of us together, they'll be back. I need time to think of a way to stop them, and I don't think they're going to let me have it.' She sonicked the wall, and the glowing plan appeared again on the old stone; Vitus stepped back in surprise, bumping his head on the column behind him, while Graham just watched with interest, business as usual. 'If this was a lair the Tenctrama used when they were at their weakest, chances are they'd have installed some sort of intruder early warning system ...'

Vitus turned to Liss. 'If this was *what?*'

'Later,' she told him, fascinated. 'But basically this entire place belongs *in* the Legion of Smoke's files.'

A sphere of light formed in front of the Doctor, showing a distorted view of the battlefield as if from a drone overhead.

'Security cameras?' Ryan ventured.

'Bird's eye view. Probably literally.' The Doctor flicked through different views of the situation outside. 'Think I've hacked into the Tenctrama surveillance feed.' She clicked and dragged with the sonic to arrange the vistas around the Hall. 'Pick a monitor, any monitor. Actually, maybe pick a few monitors each. Monitor the monitors. Choose someone to be monitor monitor and warn me if any monitor has monitored—'

'On it, Doc,' said Graham.

'With these we can keep watch on the entrance and the exits,' Vitus marvelled, 'and trespassers won't know they've been seen.'

Yaz smiled. 'Just bear in mind that we're kind of the trespassers.'

Ryan turned to Liss. 'You got any more alien weapons down here? Might come in handy.'

'There's that Arcturan grenade for a start,' Liss reminded him.

'No, no, no!' The Doctor shook her head. 'That could blow this whole place wide open!'

'Well, Vitus?' Ryan tried the jock instead. 'Besides that blaster, seen anything else that might go boom or zap?'

Vitus didn't answer, transfixed by the images of battle on the screens. 'It's uncanny,' he murmured. 'You know, Plato said, "Only the dead have seen the end of war".'

Graham snorted softly. 'Probably turning in his grave right now.'

Yaz pointed to one of the monitors. 'Doctor …'

Ryan looked, and then wished he hadn't. 'Oh, my days.'

There were Roman zombies rampaging through the camp, far from the line of battle. A wounded Strava shambled after them. They were killing the workers, the blacksmiths, stable boys, cooks, the wounded, horses and oxen, everyone and everything they could find.

'The Tenctrama have changed tactics.' The Doctor looked away, sickened. 'No notions of "sides" any more. Just kill who and what you can in one last push.'

Ryan nodded. 'Whatever they've been planning all this time, they're finally ready.'

'Talking of sides, Doctor, isn't that Attila?' Yaz pointed to another screen in the corner of the Hall. With a buzz of the sonic the Doctor made the image larger. In the confused mass of Huns, one stood under a blood-splashed banner, swinging his sword, fighting off three more men attacking with maces.

Ryan's heart quickened. 'That's not Attila, that's Bleda.'

'Bleda *is* Attila.' Yaz nudged him. 'Keep up.'

'Whoa! Well, that's definitely Alp, isn't it?' Graham chewed his lip. 'Why is Alp trying to kill Bleda – Attila I mean?'

'Because Alp died in the forest,' Yaz told him. 'You keep up too!'

'Attila *has* to stop the fighting,' said the Doctor. 'Each life that's saved sets back the Tenctrama, but his people won't retreat unless they hear it from him.' She stabbed her finger at the screen. 'Vitus, Liss, where is this taking place?'

'Close to where Ryan and I found you,' Liss answered. 'Eastern sector of the Plain.'

'His army would've seen us,' said Yaz. 'Suppose he's looking for a way in here.'

'If we're to save those soldiers we'll need a *bigger* way in.' The Doctor swept her piercing eyes around the room. 'Here's what I want you to do …'

His white mount cut down, Attila staggered away from the scrum of cavalry and climbed over the gory ruins of a Strava, pursued by three of the dead. Alp was one of them, clambering over the tusked corpse, wielding a mace.

'You dare to turn on your king?' Attila shouted. 'We were like brothers, you stubborn idiot!' He hacked the legs from under one of his attackers and smashed the second man's mace aside with the flat edge of his sword, but Alp's weapon whistled down to strike his chest. The wooden spikes didn't pierce Attila's armour but he fell to the muddy ground, winded.

Alp's walking corpse loomed over him, no triumph on its ghastly face. But then a deeper shadow fell across both of them with a whinnying cry. Attila laughed with savage satisfaction as a black horse reared up and smashed its hooves against Alp's chest, flinging him back into the bloody mêlée.

'Bittenmane!' Attila reached up for his horse's bridle and used it to heave himself back to his feet. Bittenmane's eyes were dull, his mouth dry and tacky and his flanks thick with scurf. 'No, you were never one to run from battle.'

Another corpse came shambling closer, sword raised. Before Attila could recover himself, an axe thrown from behind him came whistling past his ear and struck the man in the shoulder. Then two Roman soldiers rushed forward and set upon the Hun with swords.

Attila turned to find Aetius, at the head of perhaps fifty men, holding him at sword-point. 'Hello, old friend,' the Roman said. 'May I expect gratitude for saving your life?'

'It is you who has grown old,' Attila rejoined, 'for your wits are surely lost if you think I sought rescue.'

'Perhaps only I think clearly.' Aetius lowered his sword. 'We are all in need of deliverance, Attila. All our lives, we have waged war in order to gain advantage. Tell me, what advantage can be brought to us this day?'

Attila surveyed the fighting on the plain, the bulwarks of dead men and horses. 'There is no glory here and still less purpose,' he concluded.

'Then let me propose a truce,' Aetius said. 'A new alliance.'

Behind him, Attila recognised Thorismund, the Visigoth prince, standing bloodied but bold before a band of his shag-haired people. 'You agree?'

'I do,' Thorismund said. 'Let us work together, and quit the battlefield.'

'Spoken like a king, Thorismund.' Aetius offered his hand to Attila. 'Order your men to fall back with us.'

Attila only stared at the outstretched arm.

'Come on, you stubborn ox.' Aetius nodded to the fallen Strava. 'Let us prosecute this war as true soldiers, not keepers at the Coliseum! Outride the dead and fight for each other—'

An ear-splitting explosion roared fire up into the evening sky. Horses reared up, nostrils flaring, while many of the living fell to their knees in terror and prayed in a rain of mud and stone. Attila raised his sword in warning as a figure emerged from the dust.

It was Yasmin Khan.

'Witch,' Attila groaned, 'how you vex me!'

'Less of the witch, less of the testosterone, and faster on that handshake – please?' She put her hands on her hips. 'You don't let off an Arcturan grenade without people noticing. We need to get everybody inside.'

Attila smiled grimly. She and the Doctor were slippery witches. How had she got free from his guards? Well, perhaps he should trust to those powers of escape.

She was looking past him to where the dead were starting to advance.

'Come on!'

Another girl, pale and wearing armour, followed her out. 'There's room for everyone in the catacombs but we need to seal them up again quickly to keep out the dead, so …' She bowed to Aetius. 'With your permission, sir?'

'This one I trust,' Aetius announced.

Attila was not to be outdone. 'I trust the other – to talk us all to death if we don't act!' He surveyed the smoking hole in the ground into which the young witch was beckoning. 'I will trust the old dead in the catacombs, too. They knew when to lie down.' He climbed onto the dead Strava and raised his sword to rally his men. 'This day is backwards,' he shouted. 'The dead find life above ground, and we Huns will find life below it if we join with our enemies. For now, let us work alongside those we would kill. I order you now – let us stand together as those who would live and die only once!'

Chapter 30

The last time Ryan had played usher was on Open Day in Year Eleven when the Year Sixes came to look round their prospective new school. He'd stood outside the entrance hall giving directions to parents, most of which he'd managed to get wrong, so here was a chance to up his game. Of course, at school the way to direct people hadn't been straight through a solid wall that was glowing gold. There had also been fewer horses, but the ones like Bittenmane weren't too much trouble. 'Thank you for your service,' he told the grizzled, unkempt horse, who looked at him as if affronted.

Understandably the soldiers weren't happy about going through a shimmering barrier, but Liss demonstrated that it was safe.

Aetius greeted Vitus, who saluted him. 'I'm glad you got my message to force open the catacombs.'

'Actually, sir, I didn't,' Vitus confessed. 'It was the Doctor's idea.'

'My witch!' Attila laughed and nodded. 'She has many ideas. I may cut off her head and count them all.'

'Perhaps,' said Aetius, 'it's a good thing she wasn't killed.'
Attila grew more sombre. 'Yet.'

The dead soldiers were shambling towards them now.
Ryan fired the grey blaster that Vitus had found for him
among the piles of junk. It looked cool – proper *Star Wars*
hardware – but Ryan had already learned the hard way
that when guns were around, things could go south fast.
It's brains over bullets, he told himself. In any case, he wasn't
about to blast people even if he knew they were already
dead, so he set the gun to its strongest setting and kept
shooting the ground in front of the zombies, carving
great craters and trenches into the landscape to slow them
down.

'Keep moving!' Yaz was yelling. Licinia was sending
most of the soldiers – Huns, Visigoths, Romans, whoever
the hell they were, God knew they all stank as bad as each
other – into the cloisters beyond the main hall, the idea
being they could move on to defend the main entrance
if need be. Yaz, meanwhile, would take Aetius and Attila
straight to the Doctor like she'd asked. And as soon as the
last person was gone, Ryan and Liss were to bring down
the roof and keep out the dead.

'All right, Ryan,' Yaz called. She stood so calm and in
control between these two giants of the ancient world,
it was awesome; like they were just a couple of drunk-
and-disorderlies she'd picked up outside the Millennium
Gallery. But he knew how much doubt she hid behind that
calm expression, and felt all the more impressed. 'I'll leave
the weird impossible golden door open for you, 'kay?'

'See you soon,' Ryan said, as the three of them vanished through it. He turned to Liss and held up his gun. 'Better get filling this hole.'

'Better had.' Liss pushed Ryan backwards and fired her own gun three times at points in the wrecked ceiling. He held his ears as the rubble fell in with a booming crash, closing off the improvised exit. She slapped him fondly on the cheek. 'How's that?'

'No one likes a show-off.' He winked to show he was joking, coughed on the thick rock dust in the air, and then squinted through a crack in the pile of rubble. The dead were standing, watching, waiting. Slowly, they turned, ready to target some other survivors. Gold sparks like fireflies danced in the atmosphere above them.

'What's going to happen to all those poor people?' he said. 'Living or dead?'

She looked at him. 'Hard to tell the difference right now.'

'There's living, and there's playing at living.' He smiled at her. 'I can tell the difference.'

Liss leaned forward and held him close.

'Should we get back to the Doctor and everyone?' Ryan wondered into the side of her face.

'In a minute,' she said.

Yaz left Graham and Vitus handling crowd control in the outer gallery of the crypt to check that the Doctor was managing OK with the bigwigs of the battle – and that Attila wasn't exacting some horrible revenge for that old trick with the force-field generator. In fact, Attila was handing the thing back to her, or trying to, at least. The Doctor hadn't looked up from sonicking Liss's talk-box.

'It was a weapon that does not kill, but makes the air itself play tricks.' Losing patience, Attila dropped the generator on the altar. 'I should have expected no less from you, Witch.'

'Ooh, thanks.' Absent-mindedly the Doctor stuffed it in her pocket and continued her work on the comms-link. 'Shame that's out of power, we could really use a force field right now.' She blinked as if suddenly taking on board who had given it to her. 'Aha, Attila! Glad you made it, History's not done with you yet. And, look – *ave, ave*, Flavius Aetius. Nice to meet you.' The Doctor grabbed the general's hand and shook it, then turned to the pale youth, Thorismund. 'Visigoth prince, right? Did I call it?'

'Since the death of my weakling fool of a father, I am a king,' he replied grandly. 'Anointed in blood.'

'You Goths.' The Doctor shook her head, marvelling. '*Anointed in Blood* sounds like your difficult second album …'

Aetius's lip was curling as he gazed around the Hall with its alien relics and tech strewn about the place. 'To think I sponsor this Legion of shame. All of this should've been destroyed centuries ago.'

'Quite glad it wasn't. I'm hoping that something here could save a lot of lives.' The Doctor held out a hand. 'Talk-box, please.'

Aetius didn't budge. 'Why?'

'Because you're a good sort, really. History calls you "the last true Roman", you know. I'd hate that nice bit of puff to become a statistic.'

'Do as she asks.' Attila sounded weary. 'The alternative brings words enough to choke your strongest interpreters.'

'Very well.' Aetius handed the device to the Doctor, who had the back off it in seconds. 'This horror, this spectacle . . . it must be stopped,' he went on. 'The world must not learn of what's happened here.'

'Why d'you say that?' the Doctor wondered, wiring the talk-box into Liss's.

'Magicks erode reason. As the truth of their existence spreads, so too does fear and superstition among the people, a loss of faith in our laws, reason and governance. If the shadow of the barbarian is not to fall on our ordered world, then the common people must be protected from knowledge of magicks and the unknown.'

'By sealing it in a crypt and pretending it's not real? Fingers in your ears and la-la-la-la-la-laaa!' The Doctor demonstrated this approach. Noisily. 'How noble and enlightened. How very Roman.'

'Perhaps you are on the wrong side, Aetius,' said Attila. 'The Tenctrama have a much simpler way of keeping the populace from learning anything ever again.' His hand went to his sword hilt. 'I can show it to you, should you wish.'

Aetius's smile stayed a mile from his eyes. 'Today, I've seen enough of it.'

'But you ain't *heard* nothing yet!' The Doctor carried the comms-link lash-up over to the glowing spheres that ran the video feeds. 'I asked you here because I need you to tell your respective peoples to go home. To run away. To run and don't stop running.'

227

Attila looked appalled. 'Flee the battlefield?'

'One way of putting it,' said the Doctor. 'I prefer, starve the Tenctrama of fresh victims.'

Aetius considered. 'So, in actual fact, you propose a tactical realignment?'

'More of a strategic withdrawal,' said Attila.

'How can we command our surviving men from below ground?' Thorismund protested.

Attila nodded. 'My fastest zoltans and their horses have been slain and scattered.'

'Try this.' The Doctor waved the sonic screwdriver between the comms-link and the monitors and trails of gold appeared to join them. 'Right! Patched in audio to the communication systems, and amplified the speaker potential in the comms-link. Which means … this.' She leaned close to the cracked open communicators and spoke with am-dram passion. '*Friends, Romans, country-folk!*' The ground actually shook with the volume of her voice outside, rumbling over the plains. '*Stand by for a brief message from your generals.*' She pulled back from the communicator and looked expectantly at Attila and Aetius.

In fact it was Thorismund who stepped up to the mic first. 'Visigoths, this is your new and rightful king …'

'Speak faster,' Attila warned him. 'I wish to address my troops.'

Aetius shook his head. 'Wait your turn, my lord Attila.'

'It's no problem if you go last to order a retreat, Aetius. Romans were ever better at running …'

'Oh, the testosterone.' The Doctor looked tired, rubbing her eyes as she left them to it and crossed to join Yaz. 'Any good finds in the Legion's relic boxes?'

'Vitus found Ryan a blaster.' Yaz held out two cylindrical objects, one bigger than the other. 'And I found these.'

The Doctor blinked. 'That's a laser pointer. And that's spray paint.' She took the canisters and shook them. 'If either of these still worked, we could create a mural and highlight it with the pointer! Perfect distraction tactic.' She looked at Yaz. 'How many were you able to save from outside?'

'We got over a hundred men and maybe thirty horses before we had to close up,' Yaz told her. 'But there's so many more out there. Good idea of yours, getting them to run for it.'

'Thank you.' The Doctor was staring into space. 'I'm not sure the Tenctrama will agree.'

In the Tenctrama lair, Inkri and Enkalo listened in a cold fury as the voice of Attila rolled across the fields below like thunder.

'Like Aetius and the Visigoth, he orders evacuation of all troops,' Enkalo hissed. 'We need the dead, Inkri. We stand as the last Tenctrama, spent and exhausted. We are so close …'

'The Pit *will* be nourished. We will be renewed. Our race will spawn again.' Inkri raised her withered hands up to the darkness above. 'Let it begin.'

The slow thump of a heartbeat sounded. Enkalo's face hovered between excitement and fear as a hum of power filled the air. 'Already? But Attila has not yet been located and destroyed. Nor the Doctor and her friend—'

'Attila is isolated inside the catacombs,' Inkri hissed, tapping a long finger against her nose as golden lights sparkled through the darkness of the lair. 'We are safe to strafe the battlefield. Safe to take fresh strength – and, once restored, we shall take the catacombs – and the Doctor – by force.'

'What's happening out there?' Liss was crouched on the floor staring through the little cracks in the rubble, and Ryan knelt to join her.

The voices of Attila, Aetius and the other dude had sounded loud as launching rockets out on the plains; Ryan had been afraid they'd start another cave-in. But now something else was filling the air. Light this time.

A golden light. Faint at first, trailing around like a whirlwind, sparking, sending flares out down to the ground. Growing brighter. Stronger. Big as a town house, and getting bigger.

It slowly lowered towards the plains. As it did, lassos of light struck out from it, one, a dozen, two dozen … searing lines of power that lit the figures on the battlefield. They stood and shook and seemed to bask in the energy blast.

Liss's eyes were wide with fear. 'That light. Is it giving them power?'

'Or is it taking power?' Ryan was watching Alp, just outside, as his flesh melted into his armour, like the end of a gory snowman accelerated a thousand-fold. The lines of power were like straws stuck into the corpses, allowing the Tenctrama to suck dry whatever energies animated the remains. But it wasn't only the fighting dead affected. Dismembered bodies were struck too, severed limbs shaking as the secret essence inside them was torn free, leaving only dust.

And Ryan saw that as more and more lassos lashed out from the whirlwind of light above the plains, so the storm was changing shape: a huge, amorphous figure, stunted with no limbs, no real head, growing bigger and more malformed as it fed on the thousands of dead. Flashes of light sparked between it and the clouds above, each flash scratching off a little of the night to reveal the dark, calcified metal of the vast Tenctrama spaceship hanging high above.

'This was always going to happen, Ryan. They started planning for this day over one thousand years ago.' Liss couldn't take her eyes from the shifting horror blazing in the night. 'The Tenctrama are taking life from death. They are being reborn.'

Chapter 31

Yaz stood next to the Doctor, watching the horror blast across the battlefield, strafing the plains with supernatural light. Attila and Aetius stood beside her, staring, uncomprehending.

'The harvest,' Yaz breathed. 'Humans, animals ...'

'Even the ground is alight,' said Attila.

'That's the plant life, the insects and mini-beasts in the soil.' The Doctor chewed a fingernail. 'The natural world's been prepped for centuries, so its death will bring strength to the Tenctrama.'

Graham came back into the room, and looked visibly shaken. 'Those poor people.' He pointed to one of the monitors, where a dark stallion, rearing up at the lightshow, was struck by the lightning and disintegrated. 'That's just outside. Liss's horse ...'

Yaz took hold of Graham's hand. 'We can't stop them.'

'The Tenctrama are winning,' the Doctor breathed.

Everyone in the Hidden Hall jumped as the view on the screens changed, became a single image repeated across the monitors.

It was Inkri, shuddering in golden light, shot through with sparks. 'Winning, Doctor?' Her sibilant rasp filled the cold stone space. 'We have already won.'

'This is your last chance,' said the Doctor. 'Stop this and leave. Now. Or I'll stop you, my way.'

'Your way is to cower in hiding,' Inkri retorted. 'But why watch on monitors when you can witness our rebirth at first hand?'

The room shook, like a bunker struck by missiles high above.

'We are attacked,' said Aetius, uneasy.

'So is Inkri.' Attila pointed at the screen. 'See? She dies in fire!'

'Quite the opposite.' The Doctor shook her head. 'It's a metamorphosis.'

'She's changing?' said Graham, holding on to Yaz as the hall shook again and dust was thrown from the roof. 'Changing into what?'

'Her true form,' said the Doctor.

Inkri was groaning, gasping, her voice growing deeper. Her lined skin was falling in tatters, her golden eyes with their three pupils melting over her cheeks. The mouth grew wider, a lipless gash in a waxy, maggoty stripe of flesh. Skeletal wings twitched and flexed from her hunched shoulders in the golden firestorm.

Yaz looked across at the shrunken, mummified figure in the corner of the room. 'They don't need to pretend they're even close to human any more!'

Aetius was staring in baffled horror. 'It … it is trickery.'

'No.' The Doctor tapped the DNA manipulator. 'They only altered their form in the first place so they could fool humanity into accepting them. Influencing them through the generations, directing them to this point. Now the cycle begins again. Lives are snuffed out, and energy siphoned from the dead. That thing's being grown from the bodies on the battlefield, but it won't stop there. It'll get big enough to kill everyone clear across the Roman Empire, until the Pit is replenished, the lair teeming with Tenctrama once again.'

'And then they'll project themselves to a new world,' said Yaz, 'and trick the people there into doing the same thing.'

Graham looked pale. 'Doc, you said you'd stop them ...?'

'I will. I *have* to stop them.' The Doctor hid her face in her hands. 'Come on, think ...!'

The room shook again, so hard this time that everyone was thrown to the floor. Vitus came staggering in from the antechamber; he looked terrified.

'Something's coming!' he shouted.

'Why isn't it working?' Ryan was pacing the ground while Liss tapped at the little plate in the wall, trying to bring back the transporter interface. 'We've got to get back to the Doctor and everyone ...'

'I know! But the golden door won't open.' Liss kicked the wall in frustration and then winced. Outside, the sounds of the screaming dead and the zap of the feeding tendrils from the sky were growing louder. A soldier, trapped outside on the battlefield, started scrabbling at the rocks that had closed off the tunnel. Ryan could see through the cracks in the fall: it was a boy younger than he was.

'Please!' the young soldier shouted, desperate. 'Let me in! They're coming!'

Then he screamed as a dead Hun attacked him from behind and fell lifeless against the rocks. Both victim and killer were struck by light rays, reduced to ash as the essence inside them was drawn out.

Ryan looked away. Liss put her hand on his shoulder. 'Come on,' she said softly. 'If the transporter won't open, we'll just have to get back to the Doctor on foot, the long way round.'

A golden glow shone into the passageway and for a moment Ryan thought the transporter was back online.

But the light wasn't coming from the doorway. It was shining through the rocks from outside, and the rocks were shaking. Ryan and Liss backed away as the stones tumbled down, and a monstrous creature scuttled into their sanctuary: a giant, glistening grub with bony wings twitching on its back and long, many-jointed legs. Its eyes were stretched across the sides of its conical head, its mouth a huge hole crammed with little tongues that squirmed like maggots. There were more of the creatures outside.

Liss clutched her stomach. 'What are they?'

Bony claws extruded from the slimy skin of the beast before them, but all of them spoke together. 'We are the Tenctrama.'

'What's happened to them?' She shook her head. 'There's so many!'

'Run, Liss!' Ryan shouted. 'Run like hell!'

It was too late. The Tenctrama's wings buzzed, it slithered forward and caught Liss in its claws.

Ryan raised his gun but Liss had her own ready and fired point blank, blast after ruby blast. The Tenctrama exploded in light, and Ryan grabbed Liss by the arm, pulled her away.

The Tenctrama reformed further up the corridor, as if nothing had happened.

'They're way stronger. Run Like Hell part two, yeah? This time it's personal.' Ryan shoved Liss on ahead of him. Even as he ran after her, he could hear more of the Tenctrama slithering into the tunnel.

'The golden door is theirs.' Liss sounded frantic. 'We couldn't get the transporter working – but I think they will!'

Chapter 32

Yaz was thrown to the ground as the Hidden Hall rocked with the impact of another explosion. The Doctor didn't seem to notice, sat cross-legged on the floor, staring at the DNA manipulator.

Aetius, sweating hard, had drawn his sword – as if that could help him now. 'Those witch-monsters aim to bury us alive.'

'One way of keeping us out of their harvest,' Yaz supposed.

'Lacks the personal touch,' said the Doctor. 'More likely they're just trying to drive us outside into the open.'

'They burned up this merchant I met to nothing.' Graham looked at Aetius and grimaced. 'Sorry, chief – they did the same to your slave.'

'Consus, dead?' Aetius lowered his sword, and then his eyes, visibly affected. 'The Tenctrama killed Theodoric also. Incinerated him.'

'I'll be for it too.' Graham sighed. 'And Attila.'

'I don't fear demons,' Attila insisted, rubbing crossly at a vein pulsing in his temple.

'Where's Ryan and Liss?' said Graham. 'Shouldn't they be back by now?'

'That's a good point.' The Doctor jumped up. 'I hope they haven't found any trouble.'

Vitus came back in through the open hatchway in the stone. 'The soldiers are growing restless out there. They would rather leave the catacombs and fight.'

'And die,' said the Doctor. 'That's only going to help the Tenctrama.'

'Cowering like worms helps no one,' Attila said.

'Neither does bickering,' said Aetius, master diplomat as ever. 'Vitus, tell the men they'll see action soon enough.'

'Yes, sir.' Troubled, Vitus ducked back outside. As he did so, the glowing images in their golden spheres switched off.

'The spheres have gone dead,' Yaz realised.

'Ought to come straight back to life and start twitching, then,' Graham joked weakly. 'What's caused it, d'you think?'

'Glitch in the power flow?' The Doctor was straight out with the sonic, and coaxed a golden glow from the gloomy wall. 'Looks like the transporter went down for a time, though it seems to have fixed itself now—'

A huge, misshapen monstrosity crawled out from the golden light.

'Look out!' The Doctor sonicked the controls, and the golden glow shut down – but not before two more of the monsters had got through.

One made straight for Attila, who swung his sword; it bit deep into the pale, glistening flesh but didn't stop the beast coming. Aetius grabbed Attila and swung him out of its way just in time. It turned to tower over Aetius, a roar of anger building in its black maw – then a point of bright green light shone into the gold of its eyes and the roar became a shriek as it sank backwards, the sword still in its side. Yaz saw that Graham had picked up the ancient laser pointer in both hands and was now gripping it for all he was worth. 'Go on then,' he shouted at Aetius and Attila, 'get your men!'

As the leaders pushed past Graham for the exit, the Doctor drew the sonic and tapped it against the sword stuck into the first of the monsters. A jolt of energy sent the creature flying over the stone altar where it smashed into the wall.

'Way to go, Doc!' Graham cheered. 'What are these things?'

The Doctor was staring at the other two in fascination. 'Tenctrama, redux.'

Yaz felt a stab of fear. 'They can't stop my mind like before, can they?'

'They're like newborns,' the Doctor said, 'I don't think their own minds have moved much past the need to feed.'

'And the need to kill. Look out!' Yaz yelled as the other Tenctrama reared up over the Doctor.

The Doctor pressed the DNA manipulator to the glutinous face. 'Taking sample!' There was a spark of dark light and the Tenctrama recoiled. As it did so it was hit by staccato pulses of red light blazing into its body. Vitus was back, standing beside Graham, letting rip with the blaster.

Still holding the manipulator, the Doctor seized the distraction and ran to join Graham. But the third Tenctrama was already wriggling forward. It leapt at Vitus, its black, bony wings buzzing into flight. As it slammed into him, Graham and the Doctor were knocked aside, tumbling across the floor, but Vitus was skewered on the end of the creature's claws. He arched his back, his death scream choking away.

'No!' the Doctor shouted.

The monster pressed its maw to Vitus's corpse and made a hissing, snuffling noise that made Yaz sick to her stomach. Vitus jerked and his bones fell through his desiccated skin to fall to the flagstones as ash.

'You poor lad,' Graham whispered, shocked and stunned.

As the gorged monster reeled back, blazing with golden light, Yaz saw that the Doctor had grabbed the tin of ancient spray paint. 'Grenade!' she shouted and rolled it at the Tenctrama. It scurried backwards, as the Doctor and Graham ran for the exit. Yaz scooped up the gun and fired up at the roof, blasting the stone into rubble that crashed down on top of the monsters. She kept firing until the roof had no more stone to spit at them.

'Save the power pack.' The Doctor put a hand on Yaz's shoulder, so gentle amidst the violence. 'It must be almost exhausted.'

'Know how it feels,' Graham said.

'There's nothing we can do this time,' Yaz said, looking into the Doctor's eyes. 'Is there? Nothing.'

'We can bargain,' the Doctor announced. '*I* can bargain. For time. For something.' She crossed to the lashed-up talk-boxes and sonicked the wall to bring the comms network back online. 'This is the Doctor.' Her voice echoed back, booming and muffled, outside. 'You know I'm not from this world. You know I came here in a spaceship. Well, it can travel through time. With my help ... you won't need to play your long game any more.'

Graham looked uneasy. 'Doc? You sure you ought to tell them about—'

'Imagine if you could seed your essence, get your genetic contamination going and then jump ahead five hundred years, a thousand years ... two, three, four thousand beyond that.' The Doctor had started to pace and prowl, her voice growing louder, more impassioned. 'Think of it! Fresh harvests without the wait. Access to more advanced civilisations with weapons that can kill millions with the press of a button. I can give you that, if you let my friends here go free.'

'Doctor!' Yaz shouted, 'no!'

Then the talk-boxes blew up in sparks, and the golden glow died. The Doctor looked between Graham and Yaz. 'D'you think I got their attention?'

Yaz shivered. 'Guess we'll know soon enough.'

Ryan was running full-pelt through the gloomy catacombs behind Liss. Twice, he'd fallen over his own feet and sworn his butt off. Dyspraxics were meant to stick to long-distance running, slow and steady, but if he didn't speed up—

He fell over again. 'Damn it!'

Liss turned, panting, came back for him. 'It's all right, Ryan.'

'It's not!' he shouted. 'Keep going. I'm slowing you down. You have to get back, our people need us.'

'But what about—?'

'Go, will you!'

'You just stay on this path, all right? And follow it round.'

He nodded, and she ran on into the shadows, leaving him alone with the ancient dead. He realised his ears were ringing from all the explosions, all the shouting.

Over the high-pitched whine, Ryan heard a scuttling sound behind him. He turned.

And then he screamed, but not for long.

With a last forlorn glance at the ashes on the floor, Yaz followed the Doctor and Graham out into the dimly lit crypt. It was overrun with soldiers and horses. Attila and Aetius were barking orders in the cramped space.

Graham pulled on the arm of a statue and the stone door ground shut.

'Wait here and keep watch.' The Doctor smiled encouragingly at Graham and Yaz, and then ran to a set of mouldering stone steps at one end of the crypt and raised her arms, the DNA translator shining in one hand like the World Cup Trophy.

'Here she goes,' said Graham.

'Listen to me, everyone!' the Doctor shouted, and the room fell silent. 'The enemy's in here with us. I suspect there are more on the way. I've offered to meet with the

Tenctrama. If they go for it, I hope to distract them long enough for you all to escape. Run in different directions and spread out through the woods. Get as far as you can—'

Before she could finish, the crypt rocked as if a giant had kicked it. The tremors threw everyone to the ground. Horses bolted, trampled panicking soldiers. Graham gasped as he was knocked to his knees, dragging Yaz down with him; she shielded her face as the stone ceiling above was torn away by some incredible, invisible force.

'Doc,' Graham shouted. 'Think they heard you!'

Yaz looked up and dread filled her like cold water, her heart shrinking in on itself as she took in the vast alien light-storm dazzling down through the open roof. It twisted and convulsed in the night sky overhead, like an angry god displeased with these tiny people defiling its temple. Beyond it she saw the dark mass of the Tenctrama lair tethered to the burning sky.

Then Yaz felt her mind drifting, falling into shade, closing down. *No,* she thought, as the golden static flecked through her thoughts, *no not again*—

She heard Graham's urgent voice in her ear, saying her name, but it was too late. The Tenctrama had her.

Shielding her eyes from the glare of the Tenctrama animus roiling and writhing in the sky, the Doctor heard the shouts and screams die away, watched as the soldiers in the crypt sagged and fell still in the unnatural light. 'Oh, dear. This is the work of someone with a bit of experience. Queen of the hive time.' She straightened, braced herself. 'Inkri?'

She turned and found Ryan, bathed in golden light, suspended in mid-air above the desecrated crypt. As if pulled by poltergeists, Yaz was tugged into the air, spiralling up to join him, helpless in the soft glow of energy.

'Oh, no,' the Doctor whispered. 'Not you two ...'

'You cannot trick us, Doctor.' The image of a Tenctrama appeared, as Inkri's deep-edged voice sang from the ship above the storm, clear and no longer cracked with age. 'We have your friends. You have no hope, no defence. Surrender now to the Tenctrama.'

Chapter 33

The Doctor gazed past her levitating friends, up at the dark majesty of the Tenctrama queen. Inkri filled the sky, her true form like that of the others, projected like a hologram from the Tenctrama lair, her smile glittering in the energies of the death-storm.

'All right, Inkri,' the Doctor shouted. 'I told you, I want to deal. Don't kill anyone else – I'll help you.'

A soldier kneeling just behind the Doctor shrieked as a strand of lightning snaked out from the storm. At its touch, his body blew apart in a cloud of red particles. A nearby horse whickered and tried to bolt but it was struck too, its essence sucked up hungrily on a supernatural breeze.

'That's enough!' the Doctor bellowed. 'I said don't kill anyone—'

'You do not make terms, Doctor,' Inkri said. 'We crave the death of all organic life here.'

'I suppose the battle today gave you enough corpses to kick-start your cycle?'

'Humans provide the finest energy. Soon our storm will spread across their empire. We shall feast on the souls of all creatures from here to Rome, Alexandria, Antioch, Constantinople …'

'There's no need for that. I'll help you,' the Doctor shouted. 'I'll work with you to find a way to synthesise the energy you need from other means. You won't have to kill any longer.'

'But we *like* to kill, Doctor.' More screams from the back of the crypt and more braying of frightened horses, as strands of crackling power shot down from the sky. Yaz and Ryan shook and spun in the golden haze. 'If your friends are from the far future of this world, that would explain their genetic anomalies.'

'The synthetic fibres in their clothes prove it too. Go ahead and test them.' The Doctor looked up at Inkri. 'While you're at it, wouldn't you like to test my other friend, Graham?'

There was silence. Then a deeper light bathed Yaz and Ryan. They twitched and turned restlessly in the light as if having a bad dream.

'Of course, you can't,' said the Doctor, 'for the same reason you've sent in your newborns to get us instead of zapping from the sky and killing indiscriminately. Whoever dies gets hoovered up, and you can't risk absorbing Graham or Attila by accident, can you?'

'Doc!' Graham was backing away from the door as it ground slowly open. 'Those things that killed Vitus are coming through.'

'Ah. And they *can* discriminate. Get over here, Graham.' He ran to join her. 'Ryan and Yaz, are they all right?'

'They're being scrutinised cell by cell. It's keeping the Tenctrama busy.' The Doctor looked round, calling in a stage whisper. 'Attila? Attila, those things will be coming for you too – if you can dodge past them, get deep enough into the catacombs, maybe you can—'

'*No.*' A clop of hooves and Attila appeared from behind a thick column on Bittenmane's back. He snatched a fallen sword from the floor. 'I am Attila, the Scourge of God. Should a king who has looted half the world turn and hide?'

The pale, sticky forms of the Tenctrama burst out into the crypt, claws oozing from their massive, maggoty bodies, wings buzzing, mouths snapping open. 'Turn from those things? Hell, yeah!' The Doctor thwacked Bittenmane's hindquarters, then grabbed Graham's hand. 'Come on!'

Graham's heart was in his mouth as he ran with the Doctor up the short tunnel that led to the outside of the mausoleum. The cemetery seemed floodlit as they emerged into the wild static of the energy storm overhead. There were Ryan and Yaz, strung up by golden lights twenty feet in the air.

Graham stared helplessly. 'The Tenctrama will kill them, won't they?'

Before the Doctor could answer, there was a scatter of clip-clops on the flagstones and Attila raced past them on Bittenmane, the sturdy horse powering over the old stone like a thoroughbred tearing up the turf at Aintree.

But it wasn't fast enough.

A flex of sparking light uncoiled from the heavens, and it struck Bittenmane's chest. Graham had never heard a horse actually roar with pain before – and he would never forget the sound for as long as he lived.

'Bittenmane!' the Doctor shouted, but the animal had become ashes, sucked up by the storm. Attila, meantime, fell tumbling over the overgrown path and into the grassy graves.

'Those evil … twisted …' Graham stared, crushed and horror-struck as the Tenctrama creatures came half-scuttling, half-flying out from the mausoleum, headed for the fallen Attila. 'Doc, can't we do *anything*?'

'Nothing so well as Bittenmane.' There was new fire in the Doctor's eyes as she stared up at the undulating energy and pulled the DNA manipulator from her pocket. 'Are you ready for me, Inkri?' she shouted. 'Cos I'm ready for you!'

'No!' A scream, many voices in one, cracked out from the heavens. The whirlwind of light was flickering, and Inkri's image growing distorted. 'The Pit must not be contaminated …'

'Then you shouldn't have swallowed up poor Bittenmane, should you?' the Doctor shouted. 'Oh, yes, you scanned the humans for signs of poison, but it never occurred to you, did it – that I might have helped a lowly little horse as well!'

Graham remembered. 'Jeez, you did an' all!'

Fresh tendrils of whiteness were flailing out drunkenly from the light storm. Yaz and Ryan dropped from the sky to land like dead weights on the grass, and the Doctor and Graham rushed to their side.

'I think they're all right,' the Doctor reported.

'Course they are,' Graham said, determined to believe it. 'Will Bittenmane's poison stop the Tenctrama?'

'Afraid not. They'll simply vent the corrupted energy.' She cradled the manipulator in both hands. 'See if you can save Attila the Hun. I've got just one chance to preserve the world he wants to conquer.'

Graham looked down at the blaster he'd taken from Yaz in the crypt. Then he ran towards the slavering Tenctrama closing on Attila and yelled, 'Come on, then!'

'Come on, then,' agreed the Doctor, activating the manipulator, checking the status of the translation unit. 'Last programmed procedure, still in the memory? Yes!'

'Doctor,' Yaz said groggily.

'So glad you're all right!' the Doctor cried. 'Bit busy right now, though!'

'What's happened?' Ryan rubbed his aching head.

'Shush, quickly, help Graham!' the Doctor shouted. 'The Tenctrama have paused their renewal cycle. They're trying to isolate poor Bittenmane's DNA within the Pit ready for venting.'

'Bittenmane?' Yaz felt a pang of sorrow as she tried to shake her head awake. 'He's … gone?'

'But not forgotten! The healing gel's seen to that.'

Ryan got up stiffly. 'You mean, it's hurting the Tenctrama?'

'Not badly. There's too much fresh energy being absorbed from all over the battlefield. So, you see, I really don't have long.' The Doctor waved the sonic over the manipulator, not looking up. 'No more talk. Things kicking off. Go help!'

As she spoke, Ryan saw that Graham was trying to drag Attila clear of the fray.

'Use your hand magicks, old one!' Attila shouted, breaking his grip.

'No more juice!' Graham yelled.

Moments later, more soldiers came pouring out of the mausoleum, pursued by newborn Tenctrama; Inkri's mind control must have faltered while she coped with the emergency, but these creatures had no other focus than feeding. Aetius rattled out on horseback, trying to fend off the towering creatures as they spat lightning and fed on the corpses. Sword raised, Attila led Huns and Romans alike to help him, working together now, hacking at the monsters left, right and centre. Ryan swore under his breath, while Yaz just nodded, almost overwhelmed. This was like some full-on sword and sorcery battle, made real!

'Wait, I've still got this thing!' Graham shone his laser pointer at the Tenctrama's misshapen eyes, trying to distract them from their slaughter. Ryan had his own blaster out, and fired at the ground around the monsters while Yaz helped pull the wounded to safety. With a flood of relief he saw Liss stagger out from inside and join in the defence with her own firepower. But more Tenctrama were squeezing into view.

Whatever you're doing, Doctor, thought Ryan, *please, God, make it count.*

An outpouring of sickly green light rained down from the gunmetal mass of the Tenctrama lair in the sky.

'There it goes!' the Doctor breathed. 'Bad energy vented while new energy floods on in. So if I'm quick …' She planted the reprogrammed manipulator in the ground, pulled out the sonic and cycled through the Tenctrama wavelength signatures, the same technique as when she'd hacked into the teleport controls.

It had to work. It just had to. 'Come … on …

'Yes!'

Suddenly, the stream of bad energy flowing down from the sky was drawn across to the manipulator, like a metal rod dispersing lightning. The Doctor cried out in agony as the vortex of energy engulfed her too, but she kept twisting on the sonic, amplifying the signals, looping them.

The air shimmered, and Inkri appeared in the towering, glutinous flesh, claws clacking, spidery legs quivering as she gazed down on the Doctor, writhing in the energy flow. 'What do you hope to gain by breaking into our systems,' she mocked, 'besides an agonising death? The infected energy has been safely vented.'

'I noticed.' The Doctor smiled up at her weakly. 'So, question is, what's flooding out from your Pit now?'

Inkri twisted her head to see, and screamed in horror. 'Our energy …' A blazing stream was still being drawn down into the ground. '*All* our energy is venting!'

'You Tenctrama are linked, and so is your technology; the same basic systems—' The Doctor yelled with pain, still sonicking, willing herself to stay conscious. 'Someone clever like me can make a sympathetic resonance using this DNA manipulator and tap into your ship's systems to keep the vents open. You're throwing good energy after bad and while I control the vents, you can't …' She screamed again as the white light intensified. 'You can't stop me.'

Inkri loomed down over her, eyes narrowing, her hideous face distorted with rage. 'The energy will be collected again.'

"Fraid not,' said the Doctor. 'The manipulator … it's designed to combine your genetics with Earth-native DNA to create a hybrid – yeah?' The Doctor felt the ground tremble and buck about her. 'You've grown so obsessed with the animals you've groomed for so long, you've forgotten the *flora*.'

Inkri tried to scuttle forward but her legs seemed rooted to the spot. The grass was growing beneath her many legs, then blackening, then seething with new growth. Great roots and tendrils burst up through the smoking earth around her. 'Doctor!' she shrieked as thick stems broke through her thick white skin. 'What … what have you—?'

'I've switched out human DNA for plant DNA!' She stared up at Inkri through the blazing light as the ground squirmed with rage beneath her. 'All the energy you've gathered in your Pit, to sustain yourselves, to survive … It's pouring into the ground. Welcome to the Tenctrama's brand new life … as compost!'

Inkri couldn't even answer back. Lethal-looking thorns pushed out from under her skin, puncturing her eyes. Vines spewed from her gaping mouth and fixed her to the roiling mud as the Tenctrama life source became one with the overgrown cemetery gardens. The Doctor closed her eyes and tried to hold on through the pain, to keep the vents blocked, while the vines grew thicker and snaked blindly around her, as exotic grasses scraped against her skin, as the soil crumbled open ready to bury her alive.

Chapter 34

'What the …?' Ryan stared round, panting. One moment he'd been fighting back to back to back with Liss and Yaz, the next, the Tenctrama were collapsing into the ground, sticky hides hardening, sickly blooms bursting from their stiffening forms.

Aetius, bloodied and exhausted, backed away. 'What's happening?'

With one last great effort, Liss hurled a dagger at the nearest Tenctrama. It fell uselessly into a rustling mass of white brambles spilling out from inside the monster, plant life that quickly cracked and smoked and rotted. 'I think … they're dying.'

Panting for breath, Attila lowered his sword. 'Enough,' he commanded his men. 'She is right. It is some magick, cast by the Doctor …?'

'Look!' Yaz pointed. Ryan saw the Doctor's boots just visible through the rage of weird plant life, shooting up, growing old and dying, like the ground was clutching desperately for the sky.

'The Doc's being smothered,' Graham shouted. 'Come on!'

Ryan raced away with Yaz to help, Liss and Graham close behind them. They hacked through the blistering branches that were trying to pull the Doctor down. Ryan could hear the whirr of the sonic. 'She's still alive,' he shouted. 'Keep going!'

It was getting darker: the light storm was dying in the sky, sparking out like there was some dodgy connection in the heavens.

The sonic stopped working.

'Doctor!' Yaz shouted. She and Liss tore desperately through the dark foliage while Graham and Ryan struggled to pull the Doctor free. Graham looked up and groaned. The giant Tenctrama lair in the sky was tipping, lowering towards them, starting to fall.

'*Look out!*' he yelled, fixed to the spot in horror.

Ryan finally yanked the Doctor's arm clear of the vines, and the sonic slipped from her grip, and the Tenctrama ship plunging towards them …

Blinked out of existence.

With a final atom-splitting crack like thunder, the manipulator crumbled and the whole world shook. The vegetation around them writhed and withered. An unnatural gale blew around them and a stink of rot filled the air, like the Tenctrama were heaving out one final dying breath.

Then a new atmosphere settled uneasily over the shattered cemetery.

'Peace,' said Aetius quietly. 'Can it be there's a place for peace again in this world?'

'You talk too much,' said Attila. 'The battle is ended for now. That is all.' He threw his sword down into the scabrous plant-life. A jet black tear, like tar, oozed from the split.

'The plants are dead,' said Yaz, 'but ... they're still alive.'

'Like the Tenctrama,' said Liss.

'They *are* the Tenctrama, now,' Graham said. 'Inkri, her mates and her little ones.'

'Trapped in this form,' Yaz agreed. 'For another thousand years? That's a real living death.'

'Well, it's a cemetery, innit?' Graham managed a smile. 'At least they'll feel right at home.'

'Vitus?' Liss was looking around, frowning. 'Vitus, where are you?'

'Battle's ended,' Ryan said, crossing to join her. 'Now comes the mourning.'

Ryan was right, Yaz thought, back in the forest the following night, looking up at the stars. It was a time to mourn, and to give thanks for sacrifice. To give thanks for their lives. So many, so much had been lost: from the countless soldiers and their mounts out there on the battlefield to poor Vitus, who'd died so bravely trying to protect them. And Bittenmane, too, the sturdy mount with the shining eyes, whose sacrifice had helped to save the world.

She stood now in the remains of the clearing where they'd first met him, the land about flattened by the force-field generator, watching as survivors from the battlefield, Huns and Romans together, worked with ropes and oxen to pull the TARDIS back into a standing position so they could get inside. Aetius and Attila supervised together – they wanted the Doctor, her friends and her magicks gone from the field of battle – and while their soldiers looked drawn and harried, the two rulers had quickly recovered their calm authority.

The Doctor was quiet, sat on a cart like the one that had carried them to the Hun camp only yesterday. Her bounce was subdued, clothes blackened and skin sticky with burns. She'd spent all that day in a deep sleep, like a coma, close to death.

Don't let us lose you too, Yaz had thought, holding her friend's hand as tightly as she could. *Don't ever let us lose you.*

'She's gonna thank you for the broken fingers when she wakes up,' Ryan said. He'd been holding the other hand.

It had been at the sound of Graham's voice – or at a question only she was smart enough to answer – that the Doctor revived.

'What d'you think happened to the Tenctrama ship?' Graham pondered. 'One sec it was going to flatten us, the next …?'

'It was trying to jump back into limbo to break the venting cycle, but it couldn't.' The Doctor opened her eyes. 'I was overriding its systems with the sonic, keeping the vents open. When I stopped sonicking, the teleportation loop kicked in.' She managed a smile. 'Now the Tenctrama are out of reach, so's their ship. It'll stay lost in the gap between now and now forever more.'

'Like my brain cells when you give one of your fancy explanations,' Graham had joked. 'Welcome back, Doc!'

And it was a different world that had welcomed her. A world where the dead could rest in peace now. A world without the Tenctrama biting and scratching at the way of things. The Doctor had taken all that 'animus' pouring down from their lair and let it boil away into the cemetery gardens. The plains of Catalaunum had been razed, bare and barren for miles around, but with time they would recover.

Like all of us, Yaz thought hopefully.

'Where is the Visigoth king?' Liss asked her master, Aetius. She'd come along to see Ryan off. 'His men have left the battlefield.'

'I persuaded Thorismund that this was not the time to fight on.' Aetius gave her a lofty smile. 'He has many brothers back in the south who will also wish to be king. Better he establish himself in his own kingdom.'

Graham nodded. 'Cos if you *had* beaten the Huns, without a common enemy left the Visigoths could turn on you.'

'I get it. This way you keep a balance.' Ryan turned over a ceramic blaster in his fingers; like all the other space-age weapons, its power-pack was exhausted. 'And after all this I don't suppose anyone has the stomach for more fighting.'

Liss looked at him with a sad smile. 'Or for sticking around?'

Yaz felt bad for the girl, who'd lost so much: Vitus, their headquarters here, most of their ancient relics in the final battle, gone up in the smoke her Legion was named for.

'I've got to go, you know?' Ryan crossed to her, ungainly, awkward. 'This isn't my time, or my place. I need to be with my family.'

'In Britannia?'

'Nah.' He smiled at the Doctor, Yaz and Graham. 'Right here.'

Liss nodded, and her smile grew a little warmer. 'You will keep on chasing the darkness, won't you? While I am resolved to find brighter magicks in the world.'

'They're out there, Liss,' the Doctor told her. 'It's not all smoke and mirrors.'

'Says the witch whose life is these things and nothing more!' Attila laughed. 'It is rich, is it not, that for all your magicks, it was my splendid horse who destroyed our enemies. Attila saved you all!'

Yaz rolled her eyes. 'You'll tell us next you forced the Tenctrama to absorb poor old Bittenmane.'

'Yes! My will is absolute,' Attila claimed grandly. 'If I am to rule the world, I must have subjects.'

Aetius gave a hollow laugh. 'You certainly have a fine imagination.'

'You joke because you are afraid!' Attila marched over from where the TARDIS was being manhandled upright. 'Without an army, you cannot hold against the Huns. It is we who have the advantage over you.'

'It has been a long campaign, Attila,' Aetius said wearily. 'You have achieved your ambitions in Gaul. You have a thousand carts weighed down with loot to take back to your people. And I have kept Roman rule here in place.'

Attila smiled. 'For now.'

'What's important is that we have triumphed together over the Tenctrama and their dark magicks,' Aetius declared in full Party Political Broadcast mode. 'We have triumphed over our enemies, because it is God's will. Only through war can we divine whose cause is truly just.'

'War never determines who is right. Only who is left.' The Doctor jumped down from the cart, a little more her old Tigger self. 'Bertrand Russell said that. Over tea and scones one day. It's good, isn't it?'

'Pah!' Attila snorted. 'What's good is that you are leaving us, witch.'

Aetius gestured to the TARDIS. 'We will load your tent onto the cart and then—'

'No need! Thank you.' The Doctor ran up to the doors and pushed her key in the lock. 'Oh, and do put up a fence or something around those cemetery gardens, won't you? Keep people out … just in case.'

Yaz shivered as she and Ryan and Graham followed her to the TARDIS. Aetius, Attila and their men watched them balefully, while Liss turned and walked away into the stunted remains of the forest.

Ryan watched her go with a sigh. Yaz reached for his hand, to squeeze it, but hesitated. He took hers instead, without a moment's thought.

''Ere, Doc,' said Graham quietly, 'what happens to Aetius and Attila?'

'Both will be gone from the world within a few years,' she said. 'And their respective empires will fall apart without them.'

'So, all that fighting and killing,' Ryan said. 'It was all for nothing.'

'It's always for nothing,' she told him. 'Still. Look at them there, two mighty leaders standing together. After all this.' She smiled, blew her fringe from out of her eyes. 'History won't remember them for what they did here, but ...'

Yaz smiled too. 'It's not the end of the world.' She followed the Doctor, Ryan and Graham into the TARDIS.

'Hey! I'd better get fixing the force-field generator,' said the Doctor. 'If we were to bump into a griffon vulture during take-off right now ...'

'Don't,' said Ryan, 'just don't!'

Minutes later, wheezing and groaning like a mob of hillbillies on the mightiest moonshine, the TARDIS faded away.

Aetius stared in wonder, while Attila laughed heartily. 'Goodbye, witches,' the Hun shouted to the air, 'and may your magicks never fail you!'